**"My sister ne**  **o take care of the** **f** despair. **"She k**

"Oh, no, *chère* .... .pered. All his protective instincts surfaced at the thought that she needed him. "It's gonna be all right," he said, tilting her face up with a finger crooked under her chin.

He brushed a tear from the corner of her mouth with the pad of his thumb, then bent his head and kissed another from her cheek. It seemed only natural to lower his head another inch and settle his lips on hers.

Danielle felt all her bones melt at the exact instant Remy started to kiss her. Thoughts of nannies and demon children and her own failings flew right out of her head, and a soft, hot feeling oozed through her. "Holy smoke," she muttered when he broke off the delicious contact. Dazed, she lifted her fingertips to her stinging lips and the spot his mustache had tickled. That kiss had curled her toes . . . but it hadn't solved her problem.

"Listen, I'm sorry to have wasted your time, Mr. Doucet, but this isn't a good idea. I don't think nannies should kiss like that."

Remy grinned like a pirate. "You wanna show me how they should? I'm willing to try again."

How could she hire a nanny who kissed like a bandit, a tall, dark Cajun who made her feel breathless? "Tell me, Mr. Doucet, do you always interview for a job like this?"

His voice was as smooth and dark as *café noir*, and his smile was wicked. "You ought to see how I ask for a raise. . . ."

## WHAT ARE *LOVESWEPT* ROMANCES?

They are stories of true romance and touching emotion. We believe those two very important ingredients are constants in our highly sensual and very believable stories in the *LOVESWEPT* line. Our goal is to give you, the reader, stories of consistently high quality that may sometimes make you laugh, sometimes make you cry, but are always fresh and creative and contain many delightful surprises within their pages.

Most romance fans read an enormous number of books. Those they truly love, they keep. Others may be traded with friends and soon forgotten. We hope that each *LOVESWEPT* romance will be a treasure—a "keeper." We will always try to publish

*LOVE STORIES YOU'LL NEVER FORGET*
*BY AUTHORS YOU'LL ALWAYS REMEMBER*

The Editors

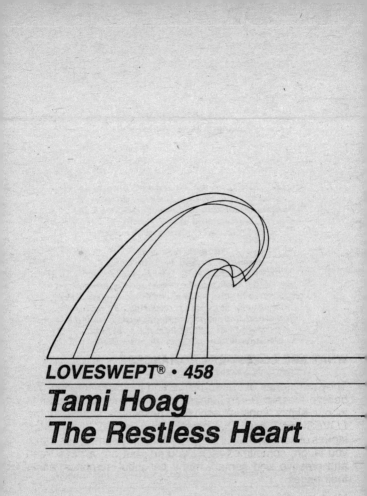

LOVESWEPT® • 458

# Tami Hoag
# The Restless Heart

*BANTAM BOOKS*
*NEW YORK • TORONTO • LONDON • SYDNEY • AUCKLAND*

THE RESTLESS HEART

*A Bantam Book / March 1991*

If you would be interested in receiving protective vinyl
covers for your Loveswept books, please write to this address
for information:

Loveswept
Bantam Books
P.O. Box 985
Hicksville, NY 11802

ISBN 0-553-44102-7

Published simultaneously in the United States and Canada

Bantam Books are published by Bantam Books, a
division of Bantam Doubleday Dell Publishing Group,
Inc. Its trademark, consisting of the words "Bantam
Books" and the portrayal of a rooster, is Registered in
U.S. Patent and Trademark Office and in other coun-
tries. Marca Registrada. Bantam Books, 666 Fifth Avenue, New York, New York 10103.

PRINTED IN THE UNITED STATES OF AMERICA

OPM  0 9 8 7 6 5 4 3 2 1

# One

"Auntie Danielle, Jeremy spit on my dessert!"

Danielle Hamilton quickly wiped a grimace of distaste from her face, lest Jeremy see it and catalog it away for future reference in his diabolical nine-year-old brain. Almost too exhausted to think, she leaned heavily against the white framed archway that led into the family room.

"Well, spit on his, Dahlia," she suggested. What did she know about kids? Nothing. She'd had an easier time of it dealing with the Bushmen of Kenya. The Tibetan nomads had been less of a mystery to her. Even as a child, she had known nothing about kids; she'd been raised in a world of adults.

"I did spit on his," declared eleven-year-old Dahlia Beauvais. "He ate it anyway."

"Gross," Danielle muttered as the doorbell rang. With a tremendous effort she pushed herself away from the door frame, side-stepping the carnage a plastic fighter jet had wreaked on a field of miniature soldiers.

"Hey, look out!" Tinks Beauvais shouted indignantly. The seven-year-old tomboy crouched behind a wing chair, poised to send a spaceship into the fray. "You're in a war zone!"

"Tell me about it," Danielle grumbled dryly.

*North and South* revisited. And this time the South was winning. One world-renown photographer from New Hampshire didn't stand a chance against this quintet of seasoned veterans in the kids-versus-adults power-struggle game. She was seriously outnumbered. They also had an age advantage she didn't care to dwell on. Their energy reserves were amazing. Hers were depleted. She was running on empty and the one person she had counted on to help her through this baby-sitting fiasco had been knocked out of commission on the first day of their mission.

She envied Butler. He was now lolling the hours away in the quiet seclusion of his quarters, happily numbed to the situation by a substantial dose of Darvon.

Lord, how the Beauvais children had rendered Butler immobile, she thought with a shudder. The indomitable Alistair Urquhart-Butler, who had run her father's household for four decades. The man who had stood the test of time, who had outlasted Laird Hamilton's five wives, and helped raise six Hamilton children, had finally been brought down by a roller skate. It was unthinkable. It was especially unthinkable because he had helped coerce her into coming to New Orleans in the first place.

"Aye, lass, I'll go with you," he'd said. "I'll lend you a hand. You can count on me."

All the counting she'd done on him so far was to count him out when he'd hit the polished pine floor with a bone-jarring thud.

As the doorbell sounded a second time, she glanced up, ignoring the intricate plaster moldings on the ceiling of the beautifully preserved Garden District home. Her interest was focused on an even higher plane. "Lord," she muttered, "this had better be the nanny or we're going to be looking at serious infractions of some of the major commandments."

I could always plead temporary insanity, Danielle thought. In fact, it had to have been some kind of temporary insanity that had allowed her to agree to stay with Suzannah's children in the first place. She usually made it a point to stay clear of children. She had to have been disoriented and confused or she never would have agreed to this. Suzannah had taken advantage of her jet lag. Her sister had pounced on her practically the minute she'd stepped off the plane that had returned her to the States after her year-long project in Tibet.

"Oh, Danielle, won't you *please* come stay with the children while Courtland and I go on vacation? They need a 'family influence.'" Danielle mocked her sister's plea as she continued down the hall toward the front door and her salvation. She gave a rude snort. "What they need is a drill sergeant."

In the hall lay an exhausted heap of brown fur that had begun the day as a large enthusiastic dog of indeterminate background. Head on his paws, he was obviously reconsidering the wisdom of moving into the Beauvais house. Danielle was reasonably certain he didn't belong there. The children had assured her he did, yet each called the poor animal by a different name. Suzannah hadn't mentioned a dog.

Suzannah hadn't mentioned a lot of things. In her haste to leave on her Caribbean vacation with her husband, Danielle's half-sister had failed to mention that her children were monsters. She had conveniently forgotten to tell Danielle that mere mention of the Beauvais house was enough to strike terror into the heart of nearly every nanny in New Orleans. After two days with her five nieces and nephews, Danielle doubted Mary Poppins would have been willing to take them on. The Beauvais children called for sterner stuff—the Marines, for instance.

She stepped over the dog and paused to take a deep breath and regroup her dwindling resources. It had taken nineteen phone calls to locate an agency willing to send a nanny to the Beauvais house. After being turned down by every place in town, she had resorted to going through the list again, disguising her voice and omitting the family name of the children. She didn't want to do anything to scare this woman off. If she didn't get reinforcements soon, she was going to have to buy a gun—for self-protection.

The ornate gilt-framed mirror that hung above the hall table told no pretty lies. Danielle groaned at her reflection. She hadn't looked this bad after two months in the Amazonian jungle. She looked like thirty-nine had come and gone several times instead of just once. Her ash-blond hair that hung just past her shoulders looked like a rag mop. Two sleepless nights of sitting up with the baby had painted purple smudges beneath her gray eyes. She had inherited her mother's classic bone structure—the world-famous Ingamar cheekbones, the slim straight nose, the sculpted chin. But what was currently arranged over it would have sent her mother, the renowned model Ingrid, into shock. Bags, shadows, and worry lines, a model's nightmare.

Remnants of the lunchtime food fight between Tinks and Jeremy clung to her lavender silk T-shirt. There were two large paw prints on her khaki safari shorts. The Hermès sandals on her feet had been painted fluorescent orange by four-year-old Ambrose while she'd attempted to feed the baby strained beets.

"This woman is going to take one look at you and run," Danielle muttered. Scrunching a handful of hair in her fist, she discovered a dried glob of beets.

"No one with an ounce of sense would come near this place."

Heaving a sigh, she pulled open the heavy oak door and her breathing stopped altogether at the sight of the person standing on the other side of the wrought-iron security door.

He was no Mary Poppins.

# Two

What a face! Danielle 's first instinct was to grab her camera and capture it on film—even though she had given up taking portraits a year ago.

Twinkling black eyes stared at her from a face that was wide, strong, and utterly masculine. Faint laugh lines fanned out from his eyes as a smile tilted up one side of his black mustache. He had a solid square jaw and bold, aquiline nose. Danielle's toes tingled. She'd always been a sucker for a man with a great jaw. A deep dimple in his left cheek revealed itself as his smile broadened. His even, white teeth flashed against his deeply tanned skin. The effect was enough to make a woman offer her services as a love slave.

His body wasn't going to change her mind on the subject either. He had the build of a heavyweight boxer—broad shoulders and a thick chest. He wore a necktie, but the top button of his shirt was undone, as if he hadn't been able to get the collar closed around his neck. Danielle would have bet her favorite Nikon that under his conservative white shirt and charcoal slacks this man was a veritable sculpture of muscle.

Her gaze drifted back to his face. "Let's run away together."

His dark eyes widened in surprise. "I beg your pardon?"

"Never mind," Danielle said dejectedly as a crashing sounded somewhere in the house behind her and reality returned with a vengeful rush. There were five little reasons she couldn't fulfill her fantasy and one *big* reason. He had to be nearly ten years younger than she was and a hundred years younger than she felt. She couldn't have run off with him; he would have had to push her in a wheelchair.

"I can't leave the house," she said flatly. "I'm waiting for a nanny—or the hardening of my arteries. Whichever comes first."

"You're Mrs. Hamilton?"

"*Miss* Hamilton," she hastened to correct him. No sense in feeling more matronly than she already did in the face of all that youthful virility. "Danielle Hamilton."

"Oh, I'm pleased to meet you, *Miss* Danielle Hamilton," he drawled, his words tumbling out of his mouth lazily, all soft vowels and Cajun French inflection. He said her name as if he already knew her—intimately. His voice was like raw silk, at once rough and smooth. His eyes glittered like polished onyx.

Danielle's toes curled against her fluorescent orange sandals. She wondered vaguely if anyone had ever formulated a theory on the voice as a sex organ. She could feel his every syllable stroking her senses. It was incredible and more than a little disturbing. She was a mature, experienced woman. She couldn't remember the last time a man had turned her bones to marshmallow with nothing more than the sound of his voice.

Holding eye contact, he reached a wide hand

through the bars of the security door. Danielle's elegant hand inched forward to meet it tentatively, as if she wasn't sure she could withstand the shock of touching him. Considering what his voice was doing to her internal temperature, she was liable to combust spontaneously if they touched.

"Remy Doucet," he said, curling his fingers around hers. The left corner of his mouth tugged upward and his dimple deepened. "I'm your nanny, *chère*."

Danielle stared at him in stunned disbelief. "I must be delirious," she said at last with a twitter of hysterical laughter. "I thought you said you were my nanny."

A delicious sexy grin spread across his face. "I am."

"You are?"

"Oh, absolutely," he said, his voice low and smoky.

Danielle shook her head, as if trying to come out of a trance. This devastating hunk of masculinity was a *nanny*? *Her* nanny? All she'd done was punch a phone number and someone had sent this piece of prime beef to her doorstep? Dial-A-Stud. What a concept!

She leaned heavily against the door frame as all sorts of illicit ideas sapped the strength from her knees. If he accepted the job, he would be in the house day and night—at Suzannah's expense, Danielle thought, a malicious smile curving her wide mouth. She would be able to look at him whenever she wanted to. The trouble was looking wasn't the only thing her suddenly crazed hormones had in mind.

She thunked herself on the forehead with the heel of her hand. Lord, she was getting the hots for the family nanny! She was fantasizing about having a handsome young man at her beck and call. What kind of depraved, nearly middle-aged person was she turning into? This was completely unacceptable behavior. She was Danielle Ingamar Hamilton, for heaven's sake! She had dated princes. She had survived jungles and deserts and life in New York City. She was known the world over for her calm, cool demeanor in every circumstance.

"You did call for a nanny, didn't you, *chère*?" Remy asked, his dark brows lifting.

"Sure I called for a nanny," Danielle said, pulling herself together. She gave him a skeptical look. "But you're not exactly what I had in mind, Mr. . . . ?"

*"Doucet,"* he finished for her, his eyes flashing with a quick burst of Gallic temper. And this job wasn't exactly what he had in mind either, lady. He was a geologist. But there wasn't a lot of work for geologists in South Louisiana these days. Things had tightened up a few years back when the oil economy had gone belly-up. He'd still had a job then. But when Eagle Oil had been absorbed by the foreign corporate octopus Knox Amalgamated, just a year ago, corporate restructuring had left him with two alternatives— relocate to the Outer Hebrides or relocate to a new profession. He had tried the first. Now he was trying the second.

"What'sa matter, *chère*?" he said defensively. "You think a man can't be a good nanny?"

"Well, no, I—"

He planted his hands at his waist and leaned forward aggressively. "You think a man would be a lousy nanny just 'cause he's not a woman?"

"Um—I haven't given the subject a great deal of thought, actually."

He shook a thick finger at her through the bars of the security door. "You think I can't be a nanny just 'cause I don't have breasts?"

Danielle cast an appreciative look at the expanse of solid male pectorals straining the confines of the white dress shirt. "Believe me, Mr. Doucet, I'm *glad* you don't have breasts. I can probably speak for all of womankind on that question."

"There's no rules against men being nannies, you know. A man can do this job just as well as a woman." His words to his sister Annick had been more along the lines of "anyone could do it," but he prudently decided to modify the statement slightly for his future employer.

"I'm sure you're right." At least Danielle wasn't about to argue the point with him. By the look of him, she figured he could probably do anything he darn well wanted to. It was kind of sweet, really, that this incredibly macho-looking guy wanted to take care of children for a living. The idea touched her in a very private, very vulnerable part of her heart.

"So, you gonna let me in, or what, darlin'?" Remy asked with a sudden irrepressible grin. His flare of temper had passed as quickly as a summer cloudburst. He leaned a beefy shoulder beside the door, crossed his ankles and fanned himself with his hand. "It's gettin' hot out here."

Not any hotter out there than it was inside her skin, Danielle thought, but she kept that little observation to herself. Remy Doucet struck her as a man who didn't need a great deal of encouragement to be outrageously flirtatious.

She unlatched the security door and, with a sweep of her hand, stood back and motioned for him to come in. As he stepped past her, her mind searched frantically for a room they could go to that didn't look like the aftermath of a nuclear holocaust. There wasn't one. Since their parent's departure the Beauvais offspring had reduced the showplace home to a shambles. They could have gone into the darkroom for the interview, but considering the man's magnetism, that didn't strike her as the brightest idea—appealing, yes, smart, no.

Remy glanced around the elegant entrance hall. Ivory silk moiré wallpaper, a chandelier of crystal prisms, a curving staircase that was like something out of *Gone With the Wind.* Nice. And despite the fact that the lady standing before him was obviously dead on her feet, there was an air of elegance about her from the top of her tousled blond head to the tips of her—fluorescent orange sandals? He frowned a bit at the footwear.

"We'll go into the salon down the hall," she said. *There's no food on the walls in there.*

Remy followed her down the hall, his appreciative gaze assessing his potential employer. She was tall, no more than a few inches shy of his own six feet, and built with the angular grace of a model. Svelte, but not skinny. Nice behind. *Really* nice behind. The kind of legs that haunted a man's most erotic dreams. He wondered if they were as silky as they looked. He flexed his fingers at the thought of running them down those long limbs.

Hold it back, Remy, he warned himself, the lady's gonna be your boss.

*Well,* said the little devil on his shoulder, *lookin's no sin.*

As usual, he took the devil's advice with a grin.

As they drew even with an archway a blast of rock music hit them with the force of a hurricane wind. Jeremy leaped out of the hall closet directly in front of Danielle, a nylon pulled down over his face, mushing his features grotesquely. Danielle shrieked and flung herself back up against the wall, banging into a narrow Louis XIV table and overturning a cobalt vase of fresh flowers. Tinks dashed out of the family room with a replica Uzi propped on her hip. She executed a neat shoulder roll and came up behind a startled Remy. Using his muscular legs for cover, she took blind aim at her brother and shot a staccato burst of grape Kool-Aid across the hall that left a wet purple trail on the floor.

Before Danielle could do anything more than holler their names, the marauders vanished out the front door. Her heart sank. There was little doubt in her mind Remy Doucet would now take his gorgeous body and his child-rearing skills and head straight back to the nanny agency from whence he had come. He had a rather shell-shocked look about him at the moment. As soon as he came around he would bid her adieu and vamoose like any sane, sensible person.

A sudden sense of panic gripped her. She didn't want him to go. He was the only adult she'd been able to find who was brave enough or foolhardy enough to set foot inside the Beauvais house. What was she going to do if he took off? She would be left alone again with *the children*. Goose bumps raced over her flesh. The children would be left alone with *her*. The combination was toxic.

She leaned in the family room doorway and shouted at the top of her lungs. "Dahlia, turn that stereo down or you won't live long enough to find out what 'I Want Your Sex' means!"

Dahlia flipped a knob on the stereo and sauntered toward her aunt with a smug look. She flipped her long copper hair back over her shoulder and said, "I already know."

Danielle turned to Remy with a pained smile and gave him one of Suzannah's most famous lines. "They're such spirited children."

Remy ducked his head and cleared his throat.

"Who's the hunk?" Dahlia asked, eyeing him with outrageous audacity.

"I might be your new nanny," Remy said, trying to look stern. He was fairly certain the nanny training manual would take a dim view of being amused by impudence.

Dahlia grinned. "Radical!"

Danielle turned the girl by the shoulders and nudged her back into the family room. "Why don't you go browse the catalogs for training bras, dear?"

"I want the push-up kind. Like Madonna has." Dahlia dropped to her knees and dug through the rubble on the coffee table for a catalog. "Molly Gerard's mother ordered her one just like this." She glanced up out of the corner of her eye to see how well her story was being received.

Danielle gave her a look. "Right. Nice try."

Remy looked over the girl's shoulder, his eyebrows bobbing up at the sight of a red lace bustier. He glanced askance at Danielle. "She's got good taste."

"Small consolation," Danielle muttered dryly. "She may not live to make use of it."

A floor above them a baby began to cry. The sound came in a kind of stereo effect, crackling over the monitor Danielle wore hooked to her beaded belt and wafting down the stairs. To her extreme horror, Danielle's eyes suddenly brimmed with tears. She was exhausted. She was frustrated. She was secretly terrified of babies. Why, oh why had she let Suzannah talk her into this?

Biting her lip, she stepped past Remy with her head down, her hair shielding her face from his curious gaze. She took the stairs two at a time, her hand skimming up a mahogany banister that was dull with sticky fingerprints. She could hear Remy's footsteps right behind her.

"How many are there altogether?"

"Five."

His eyebrows shot up. She didn't look like the mother of five. Nor did she seem particularly well equipped to deal with five children. But then this was a swanky part of town. Danielle Hamilton didn't have to be well equipped for motherhood. All she needed to be able to do was dial the phone so she could hire someone else to handle the task. Anger flared through him. He was of the firm belief that people shouldn't have kids if they didn't know how to love and care for them.

Putting a tight leash on his opinions, he said neutrally, "Raisin' five kids all alone must be some kind of job, eh?"

"Alone?"

"You're divorced, right?"

"Me? I've never been married."

Disappointment settled over Remy like a thick mist. Five kids and she'd never been married? That was a hell of a track record. He whistled between his teeth. "Ah, me, *chère*, you get around."

Danielle wheeled on him at the door of the nursery, her eyes like twin silver moons. "Me? You think these are *my* kids? You've got to be kidding!"

Remy stared at her, confused but relieved. "They're not your kids?" he asked above the wail of the baby.

"No, thank God. I'm only here because I'm a sucker. These little darlings belong to my sister, Suzannah Beauvais. She and her husband are allegedly on vacation. Personally, I think they've skipped town. Who ever heard of rich people going to the Caribbean in the dead of summer?"

Remy shrugged, deciding to treat it as a rhetorical question. He didn't know all that much about rich people.

Danielle shook her head in disgust as she crossed the plush rose-colored carpet to the white crib where little Eudora sat alternately bawling and choking herself with her fist. "She wanted me, of all people, to stay with her children as a family influence while she and Courtland are away. I'm sure if she ever does come back she'll be prosecuted to the full extent of the law."

She stared down forlornly at the sobbing baby, wondering how she was supposed to know what Eudora's problem was. She had absolutely no clue how to go about deciphering the moods of a ten-month-old baby. What a failure she was as a woman, she thought as two big fat tears rolled over Eudora's lashes and down her cheeks.

Remy scooped the baby up, cuddling her close and murmuring to her in Cajun French. She was a cute little thing. Twenty pounds of baby fat with big blue eyes and fuzzy red hair. With one hand Remy found a soft terry-cloth elephant stuck down in one corner of the crib. He handed the toy to Eudora, who promptly began gnawing on the elephant's trunk. The baby's wails immediately died down to whimpers, then segued into contented cooing and intermittent hiccups.

Danielle gave him a wary look, as if she'd just witnessed an act of witchcraft. "How did you do that?"

"It's all done with mirrors," Remy replied. What kind of woman didn't know enough to comfort a teething baby? What kind of mother would leave her children with someone who was so obviously lacking in any maternal instincts? His temper surfaced again and he vented it on Danielle, momentarily forgetting that she was his prospective employer. He was much more used to giving orders than taking them. "She's cuttin' teeth. Don't you know enough to give her something to chew on? What kind of a baby-sitter are you?"

"I'm no kind of baby-sitter!" Danielle snapped, frustration pressing against the backs of eyes in the form of hot tears. "I'm just supposed to be the family influence. Butler is the baby-sitter, dammit, and where is he when I need him? Felled by a roller skate! I don't know anything about babies! How was I supposed to know they don't come with teeth included? That's what I'm hiring you for!"

Remy felt a stab of panic as Danielle turned her back to him and started to cry very quietly. It was just a gentle sniffling, a slight trembling of her shoulders. Exactly the way he had always imagined classy ladies would cry. But it was one thing to quiet a baby. A full-grown woman was something else altogether. He could hardly placate Danielle by sticking a terry-cloth elephant in her mouth.

He set Eudora back in her crib and went to stand behind Danielle, not sure what he should do. It tore him up inside to hear a woman cry. To know he was the cause of those tears was like salt on the wound. He doubted most trained nannies would take their boss in their arms and hold them, but that was what he wanted to do. It was the only thing he could think to do.

"Don't cry, *chère*," he begged in a low, smoky voice, turning Danielle gently by the shoulders. He gathered her up against him, stroking a big hand over her soft mane of angel hair, drawing her head down to his shoulder. She stood as stiff as a rail against him, fighting her tears and the comfort he tried to offer. "I'm sorry, darlin'. I shouldn't have gotten after you like that."

"I'm—doing the—b-best I—c-can!" she said with jerky indignation. "I—c-can't help it—I d-don't know any-thing!"

"Course you can't, sugar," Remy murmured, secretly baffled at the prospect of a woman who was not adept at handling babies.

"I—I'm t-tired and fr-fr-frust-strated."

"Sure you are."

"And I've g-got—beets in my hair!"

It was that final small indignity that made the tears gush forth in a tidal wave. It had been ages since Danielle had cried in front of anybody. She had always found those rare occurrences embarrassing, undignified, and well beneath her powers of self-control. But the horse was out of the barn now. There seemed no point in trying to hold back. Besides, she didn't think she had the strength to stem the flood. She hadn't had a wink of sleep in over two days and it felt so darn good to have someone to lean on, if only for a few minutes.

Remy's eyes misted over as he felt Danielle let go of her pride and sag against him. "Aw, you just put your pretty face on ol' Remy's shoulder and cry it all out, darlin'."

He stroked her back with a slow steady hand, sympathy seeping through him. The poor thing. Why had she taken on this job when she admittedly had no experience with kids? It was a well-known, scientifically documented fact that kids could sense that kind of thing and mercilessly rode roughshod over rookies. Poor Danielle.

Oooh, he liked the way her name sounded in his mind—kind of soft and sexy. It was the kind of name that would roll easily off his tongue during lovemaking, sounding dark and erotic. He liked the way she felt against him too. Their bodies were instinctively curving into one another, finding all the places where they fit perfectly, like two pieces of a puzzle. Desire sluiced through him like a hot lazy river.

"They won't listen to me," she mumbled, her face still squashed against his brawny shoulder.

"I know they won't," he murmured, his lips teasing her silvery hair.

"It's not that I don't like kids. I used to be one once."

"Sure you were, *bébé*." But she wasn't anymore. She was a woman, and a damned appealing one.

"Suzannah never should have asked me to help," she said, her heart filling anew with despair. "She knows I'm terrible at this."

"Oh, no, *chère*, no," he whispered as she hiccuped. "It's gonna be all right, you'll see. I'm here now." Every protective instinct Remy possessed surfaced at the thought that she needed him. He was a man who had always respected and acted on his instincts. "It's gonna be all right," he said again, tilting her face up with a finger crooked beneath her chin.

Danielle looked at him as though he were the only man left on earth and the two of them had been designated by God to perpetuate the species. *Bon Dieu*, but she was pretty, even with beets in her hair.

He brushed a tear from the corner of her mouth with the pad of his thumb. Then he bent his head and kissed another from her cheek. It seemed the most natural thing in the world to lower his head another fraction of an inch and settle his lips against hers.

Danielle felt all her bones melt the exact instant Remy started to kiss her. All thought of nannies and demonic children and her own inadequacies flew right out her head, leaving behind bright bursts of star dust and gold dust and a soft, hot feeling that oozed through her and settled low in her belly. She pressed herself closer to him as her lips parted, inviting him to deepen the kiss, but Remy moved back a fraction of an inch and raised his head instead, breaking off the delicious contact.

Danielle felt as if she were going to crumble to the floor like so much discarded clothing. "Holy smoke," she muttered, staring at him. Dazed, she lifted her hand to touch her fingertips to her stinging lips and scratch at the spot his mustache had tickled. That kiss had curled her toes. She'd heard bells. Some welcome to the neighborhood. She doubted Mr. Rogers had ever kissed anybody like that.

"I don't think you're old enough to kiss like that," she said, instantly annoyed with herself for raising the subject of age.

"I been outa short pants a long time, sugar," Remy assured her.

"Oh, yeah? I'll bet you don't know who the Shi-rells are."

"No," he admitted. "Do you know the Balfa Brothers?"

"No."

He shrugged. "Then we're even."

"Even? Huh," Danielle huffed, crossing her arms over her chest. She scowled at him, her straight dark brows pulling together. "How old are you, anyway?"

"Thirty-one. How old are you?"

"I'm—" She gave him a narrow-eyed glare. "None of your business."

"Oh, come on, sugar, you can't be—what? Thirty-five, thirty-six?"

Danielle couldn't decide whether she should be flattered or offended. It seemed like a good time to change the subject. Age wasn't going to be relevant at any rate, because she most certainly wasn't going to get involved with him.

"Listen, I'm sorry to have wasted your time, Mr. Doucet, but this is a really bad idea. I don't think nannies should kiss like that."

Remy grinned like a pirate. "You wanna show me how nannies should kiss? I'm willing to try again."

Danielle stepped behind a white rocking chair as he took a step toward her. "I appreciate your enthusiasm, Mr. Doucet—"

"Remy," he corrected her with a tsk-tsk.

Danielle swallowed hard. "Remy." Just as she had feared, his name sounded sexy even from her own lips. It tasted sexy. Just saying his name recaptured the rich dark flavor of his mouth. "No offense, but doesn't your agency have any stout ladies with iron-clad hairdos and support hose?"

"Sorry, *chère*," he said with a devilish sparkle in his dark, dark eyes as he stepped around the rocker and trapped Danielle against it with an arm on either side of her. "We're fresh out of them little blue-haired ladies."

"How about one of those pudgy Aunt Jemima types?"

He shook his head, his inky hair tumbling into his eyes. "All gone."

Danielle thought her heart was going to pound its way right out of her chest. Remy stood close enough for her to see the shadow of his afternoon beard darkening the broad plane of his cheek. How could she hire a nanny who kissed liked a bandit and had to shave twice a day? But there he stood—tall, dark, and Cajun, with three wayward locks of unruly black hair falling across his forehead and the wickedest bedroom eyes she'd ever seen. Just looking at him made her want to rip his shirt open and run her hands through his chest hair.

It occurred to her that this whole scene was preposterous. She wasn't the kind of woman who succumbed to instant attractions. In fact, she had pretty much decided to steer clear of men altogether after her last relationship had fizzled. It had become apparent to her that, like many a Hamilton before her, she was doomed to nothing but failed romances. That was a fact of life better accepted than fought against. Besides, this man was applying for a domestic position. She had been raised to think it was unseemly to chase the hired help.

Of course, she wasn't the one doing the chasing now. She eyed Remy warily as he inched a little closer. He was staring at her mouth as if it were nature's most fascinating phenomenon. Anticipation rippled through her.

"Tell me," she said, sounding breathless instead of droll. "Is this the way you normally interview for a job?"

One side of his mustache hitched up and his dimple cut deep into his cheek. His voice was as smooth and dark as *café noir.* "You oughta see how I ask for a raise."

Danielle felt her stomach drop all the way to her fluorescent feet.

"How many other people you got coming to interview for this job?" Remy asked, forcing himself to take a step back away from her. It was a wonder she hadn't bonked him on the head with something and run to call the cops. He was coming on like a caveman. But then she made him feel a little primitive. The idea of tossing her over his shoulder and carrying her off into the bayou country held an undeniable amount of appeal.

Chemistry. That's what was going on here, he decided. He was a man of science, he knew all about chemistry and the irresistible forces of nature . . . and instincts and biology and birds and bees and beautiful ladies with big pewter-colored eyes. . . .

She dodged his gaze and nibbled on her lip, obviously contemplating a fib.

"How many?" he asked again.

"Um . . . a few," Danielle hedged, sucking in a deep breath.

Remy shrugged. "One? Two?"

"Give or take."

"Give or take how many?"

She scowled at him. "One or two."

"See there, angel," he said, wagging a finger at her. "You gotta keep me. I'm all you got."

An interesting thought, Danielle conceded as an ominous thud sounded a floor above them. She'd run out of agencies to call. The next names on her list had been a voodoo priestess and a professional alligator wrestler.

She shot a glance at Remy, who had gone back to the crib to check on Eudora. Like magic, the sexual tension that had hung thick in the air had vanished. She wondered wildly if she had imagined it. Maybe it had been a combination of exhaustion and wishful thinking. Practical though she was, she wasn't above fantasizing about handsome, virile men with more hormones than sense. In fact, as forty loomed on the horizon like a black cloud, she could probably count on a lot of moments of temporary lunacy concerning such things.

"How long are the parents gonna be gone?" Remy asked. He picked the baby up and tucked her under one arm like a football as he began snooping around the well-equipped nursery.

"Three weeks," Danielle said absently, frowning. "Are you sure that's how you're supposed to carry a baby?"

"Oh, absolutely." It seemed the most natural way to tote a baby for a man who had gone to LSU on a football scholarship. He reached his free arm into the small white linen cupboard that was situated in one corner of the blue-walled nursery as he lied smoothly. "It's the first thing they teach us at nanny school."

"Oh. Well . . ."

Eudora squealed in delight, lending credence to Remy's questionable statement. She stuck her arms out like a miniature flying Supergirl and said, "Brrrrph!", spraying drool in all directions.

Danielle grimaced. "They wanted a second honeymoon to celebrate the fact that Suzannah is the only Hamilton in nine generations to have a marriage last more than five years. We're cursed, you see."

Remy shot her a suspicious look. "Cursed? Like black magic?"

"Cursed, like a good old-fashioned Scottish curse," she explained. "I don't ordinarily believe in that kind of thing, but there's plenty of documentation to back it up. A rival clan chieftain put a curse on Ramsay Hamilton in 1516 for stealing his bride. We've basically been failures in marriage ever since. So I guess Suzannah is justified in wanting to celebrate. She and Courtland have made it twelve years.

"Personally, I think three weeks is a little excessive

as honeymoons go. I mean, how many different ways can you really . . .ah . . . well . . ." She stammered to a stop and blushed furiously.

Remy turned suddenly and leaned down close to her. "Come on, Danielle," he said in that sandy warm voice. "Where's your sense of romance? Wouldn't you like a three-week-long honeymoon?"

"Sure," she quipped, her head swimming. "Where do you want to go?"

His voice dropped another rough note from satin to black velvet. His gaze caressed her lips. "I'd take you to heaven, angel."

"They'd never let you in," she managed to murmur as shivers washed over her skin.

He chuckled, a deep, masculine sound that rumbled up from his chest. "No, but then it's the gettin' there that's all the fun, eh?"

The man was incorrigible. Here he stood, his future in her hands and a baby in his own, and he had the audacity to flirt with her shamelessly. She might have been offended if she hadn't been so close to having a birthday. The fact of the matter was she liked Remy Doucet a lot. Probably too much.

"Here," he said, flipping off the animal magnetism again as easily as he'd turned it on. "Take the baby."

He thrust Eudora into her arms and Danielle latched on to the poor child with all the awkwardness of inexperience and blind terror. She juggled the baby like an overloaded grocery bag.

"Be careful," Remy added as an afterthought just as Danielle managed to squeeze the baby up against her. "She's soakin' wet."

"Ugh!" Eudora was immediately thrust an arm's length away. She gurgled and kicked her feet merrily in the air. Danielle stared down at the big wet stain on the front of her lavender silk T-shirt and spoke through her teeth. "When Suzannah gets back I'm going to commit unspeakable atrocities on her person. And then I'm going to get *really* mean."

Remy frowned as he took the baby and put her on the changing table. "I take it you're not so happy with any of this business."

"It's not that I don't like kids," Danielle explained. "They're fine as long as they don't throw up or wet on me or have criminally insane minds. Unfortunately, that leaves Suzannah's kids totally disqualified."

Remy clucked as he changed Eudora's diaper. "They can't be that bad."

"Did you ever see *The Omen*?" she asked casually as she plucked her soggy blouse away from her skin. "I suppose I might be exaggerating. I don't have much experience with kids. My mother divorced my father when I was two. I was raised mostly on fashion shoots. If you need someone to baby-sit a temperamental model or placate a high-strung photographer, I'm your girl. But when it comes to babies . . . I'm not so good."

Her voice thinned and trailed off, and Remy noted with interest that her gray eyes darkened and a shadow passed over her features like a storm cloud as she glanced away from him. She suddenly looked sad and lost. Her fingers toyed nervously with the fringe on a knitted afghan that lay folded over the back of the rocking chair. He sensed there was more to the story than she was telling, and he knew an intense desire to have her confide in him, though he doubted she would.

"So you've never stayed with your nieces and nephews here before?" he asked, sounding vaguely amazed. It seemed his life was constantly overrun with little relatives.

"No," Danielle admitted, annoyed that she should feel even a pinch of guilt over that. They weren't her children. She wasn't responsible for them. That was a fact that should have made everybody breathe easier. "I travel a lot in my work. I've just returned from a year-long stay in Tibet."

"Tibet?" Remy echoed, his face the picture of distaste. He plopped the baby down in her crib and handed her elephant back to her. "You got family there?"

"In Tibet? Of course not."

"And you stayed there for a year?"

Not liking the disapproval she thought she saw in his dark eyes, Danielle turned the conversation back in the direction it should have been going all along. "So, how long have you been a nanny?"

"Oh . . . not long . . ." he mumbled, head down as he went to the little white porcelain sink set in the counter beneath the linen cupboard. He devoted what seemed to Danielle to be an inordinate amount of attention to washing his hands.

"I suppose I should ask to see your résumé or references or something."

"Oh . . . darn . . . I guess I forgot my résumé," he said, hoping she might forget about it too. "I've got lots of experience, though, and I did remember to bring the agency agreement along."

He dried his hands on a little pink towel, then dug a folded two-page form out of his hip pocket and handed it to Danielle. She dragged her eyes away from the spot where his fly had snugged up against a very impressive part of his anatomy and took the form, just barely resisting the urge to fan herself with it.

"Actually, I don't think we'll be needing this," she said in a high, breathless voice. She sent Remy a brittle smile and tried frantically to rally her common sense. She really couldn't keep a nanny who unleashed mad desires in her. "You just don't quite fit my needs at the moment."

"Sure I do, sugar," Remy drawled, backing her up

against the rocking chair again. "That's the problem, isn't it? Maybe I fit your needs a little too well?"

Danielle tried to talk around the heart that was suddenly lodged in her throat. Her eyes fastened on the masculine curve of his lower lip and her palms started to sweat. "I don't know what you mean."

"You hadn't ought to fib, angel. That's a bad example for the little ones."

He moved back a fraction, giving them both room to breathe. He needed this job. He needed the money, for one thing. But overshadowing that practical reason was a lady with quicksilver eyes and hair like winter moonlight. More than the job, he wanted the chance to explore this volatile chemistry that simmered between himself and Danielle Hamilton. While he was at it he could certainly manage to take care of a few little kids. The first thing, though, was to get the position, and he wasn't exactly doing a great job of that. It didn't take a genius to see Danielle was nervous about the attraction pulling them together. It was the reason she was trying to push him away.

He sighed and ran a hand back through his hair. Putting on his most contrite expression, he said, "Look, *chère*, you need a nanny and I need a job. I promise you, I'm good with kids and I'll be on my best behavior."

"That's probably not saying much, considering what I've seen so far," Danielle said, folding her arms defensively over her chest,

"I'm not gonna lie to you and tell you I'm not attracted, sugar, 'cause I am. But like I told you, I need this job and you need a nanny. Who else you gonna call?"

"Well, Rambo was next on my list."

A small figure wearing a Ronald Reagan mask suddenly appeared at the door of the nursery. Bright orange hair stuck up like a rooster's comb above the mask. Below it was a pair of rumpled Spiderman pajamas. There was a ragged, dirty black and white stuffed dog tucked under the child's right arm.

"Auntie Dan-L?"

"Hi, Ambrose." Danielle smiled warmly at the four-year-old. "What's happening?"

"Jeremy's hanging Tinks from the roof by her feet."

# *Three*

Remy paused outside the front door of the Savoy Agency to pull himself together. The agency was housed in a narrow three-story red brick building built during the last days of the French rule of New Orleans. Like the others that crowded shoulder to shoulder along the street, it still gave all the appearances of being an elegant town house with its black lacquered front door and shutters and the delicate ironwork balconies that graced the second and third floors. Only the polished brass plate on the door gave any indication that a successful business was conducted behind the quaint façade.

Remy straightened his tie, slicked his hair back with his fingers, and took three slow deep breaths. *Bon Dieu,* those Beauvais kids were monsters! Damned if he was going to admit that to his sisters, though. He pasted on a brilliant smile that lit up his dark face, pushed the door open, and sauntered into the air-conditioned cool as if he'd just come from a refreshing walk through Audubon Park.

The interior of the building was every bit as gracious as the exterior. Burgundy velvet drapes hung over white sheers at the tall window in the reception area. Two camel-backed sofas in the same color invited clients to sit and browse through the magazines scattered over the walnut coffee table. The overall effect was of understated elegance only slightly broken by the pink beanbag chairs and assortment of toys that were nestled into one corner for clients' children.

Remy's younger sister Annick sat behind the delicately carved walnut reception desk with the telephone receiver sandwiched between shoulder and ear. Two thick books lay open on the desk before her. She scribbled in a spiral notebook as she spoke, effectively dividing her attention between the call and her studies in the way only a harried law student can. As she glanced up at Remy, she smiled and brushed her black bangs out of her dark eyes with the eraser end of her pencil.

He spread his arms wide and executed an ambling pirouette as if to say "Here I am, and in one piece yet." Annick bid her caller goodbye and hung up the phone, never taking her eyes off her big brother. Remy perched a hip on the corner of the desk and stuck his hand out, palm up. "Fork it over, *'tite soeur.*"

"What?"

"What! The twenty bucks you owe me, that's what."

"I don't know what you're talkin' about. You don't, either, if Giselle asks you. I already got the sharp side of her tongue when I told her you'd gone out. You were supposed to work the desk until four."

"I couldn't very well do that and prove to you what a good nanny I could be at the same time, now could I?"

Unconcerned by her warning, Remy pulled the agency agreement out of his pocket and handed the crumpled papers to Annick. "I am now officially the Beauvais family nanny. Here's your proof, darlin', signed, sealed, and delivered."

Annick unfolded the forms, her pretty mouth turning in a frown of distaste. "This is filthy! What's all this here down at the bottom?"

Remy glanced away, rubbing a hand across his mouth as he grumbled. "Um—that's nothin' much, there. Just a little blood, that's all."

"Blood? Yours, I hope," Annick sassed. "You a nanny. Talk about!"

Her mocking laughter cut off abruptly and she winced as the door behind her flew open and Remy's twin sister Giselle stormed out of her office, blustering like a human hurricane. Her black eyes flashed as she rounded the desk and planted her hands on her nicely rounded hips. She may have been dressed like a businesswoman in her fitted blush-pink suit, but her expression was more that of a tag-team wrestler.

Both Remy and Annick instinctively leaned back away from her as she let loose a string of backwater Cajun expletives that singed Remy's ears. When she switched back to English, her temper thickened her accent and eroded the proper grammar she normally used.

"What'sa matter wit de two of you? You tryin' to ruin my business or somethin'? Me, I got a fine reputation in this town, no thanks to the likes of you! Annick, you coverin' for Remy while he goes out masquerading as one of my nannies. What he knows about babies, that one, you couldn't feed a crawfish!" Giselle wasn't in the least softened by her brother's hurt-offended look. "And you!" She jabbed his sternum with a neatly manicured forefinger. "You oughta know better. You ain't a nanny, but you sure oughta have one!"

"I got the job," Remy said softly.

Pacing back and forth in front of the desk, Giselle ranted on. "Impersonatin' one of my nannies! My nannies are de finest in all of N'Awlins—trained, experienced—" She brought herself up short and stared at him suspiciously. "You what?"

He picked up the agency agreement Danielle had signed and waved it, a smile of smug satisfaction lighting up his handsome face. Giselle snatched it away from him and studied the document with the critical eye of a business-school graduate, grimacing at the ratty state the thing was in. "What did you do to this, *cher*? Run over it with your car?"

Getting run over by his car was about the only indignity the contract had escaped. It had been to the roof of the Beauvais house where he had rescued Tinks from Jeremy's evil clutches and been kicked in the shin for his troubles. Ambrose had tried to feed the form to the dog, who had opted to bury it in the rose garden. Remy had extricated the thing from under a freshly fertilized bush that was mostly thorns, and had bled all over it before he could hand it to Danielle for her to sign.

"The only thing that counts is the bottom line," he grumbled.

"No matter." Giselle shook her head, her fashionably bobbed black hair swinging around her face and falling neatly back into place. "You got no training, you got no experience—"

"I got plenty of experience!" Remy argued. "How many times have I taken care of your kids? Or Alicia's? And how about cousin Emile's boys? I've looked after them plenty."

"Well, yes, but—"

"It's the Beauvais house," Annick said with appropriate awe as she tapped at the agency agreement with the end of her pencil.

Giselle's eyes widened in disbelief. "What?" She jerked the form back up in front of her face and read the line twice. "I told that woman we didn't have anybody to send there."

"She gave the name Hamilton when I talked to her," Annick said.

"Huh! I'll bet," Giselle snorted. "She must have gone through every agency in the book, found out no one was crazy enough to send a nanny to that house, then started all over again with an assumed name. Of all the low—"

"It wasn't exactly a trick." Remy jumped to defend Danielle, then purposely relaxed as his twin's keen eyes fastened on him a little too intently. With studied nonchalance he asked, "So, you got anybody else you'd send there?"

"I wouldn't send the devil himself to that house."

"Remy's the next best thing," Annick said with a giggle. He slanted her a look and pinched her cheek.

Giselle's expression was apprehensive. "You sure you want to do this, Remy?" she asked, as if he were volunteering for a suicide mission.

He gave a lazy shrug that said it didn't matter much to him one way or the other, while visions of Danielle danced in his head. He could still taste her, sweet and warm on his lips. He could still see the look of unabashed wonder in her eyes as she had recognized the electricity that hummed between them. He could still sense the sadness and uncertainty in her when she'd told him she wasn't much good with kids. Was he sure he wanted this job? Was he sure he wanted to spend day and night in the company of Danielle Hamilton? What a question!

"I'm good with kids." Grudgingly he added, "I need the money."

Giselle patted his cheek and gave him the same look of sympathy she would have given one of her own children. "I know you do, *cher*."

She had hired him to help answer the phone while her regular receptionist was on maternity leave, but that wasn't much of a job as far as pay or prestige went. Her brother was a proud man. He didn't like the position he'd been put in by unemployment. He hadn't complained, but Giselle knew. As twins, there was a level of communication between them that needed no words.

She nibbled at her lush lower lip. "Well, it's a sure thing that woman isn't going to find anyone else to help her. And you *are* good with the little ones. I guess the job is yours, if you really want it."

Remy barely managed to keep from leaping up and dancing his sister around the room. He thanked her with his smile.

Giselle picked up the agreement again and studied it more closely. "Who is this Danielle Hamilton? Why didn't Mrs. Beauvais sign this?"

"Mrs. Beauvais is away on a second honeymoon with Mr. Beauvais. Danielle is her half-sister. She agreed to stay with the kids, but—"

"*Danielle*, is it?" Annick questioned, brows lifting above wickedly sparkling dark eyes. She leaned over the desk and poked him with her pencil. "Who is this Danielle, Remy? Is she pretty?"

He shrugged and dodged his sister's teasing look, but he couldn't stop the flush that rose up from his shirt collar. *Bon Dieu*, he felt like a teenager caught staring at his secret sweetheart. It was on the tip of his tongue to say that Danielle was a shrew-faced hag. Of course, it was too late for that; his blush had given him away.

Giselle crossed her arms over her chest and tapped a pink pump on the sensible flat gray carpet. She drilled her twin with a look that discouraged prevarication. "Oooh, now we get to the heart of the matter, eh? You want to take this job because of *une belle femme*?"

Remy scowled. "She needs help."

"*Mais non, 'tit frère*, you gonna be the one needs help if you damage the reputation of my business tryin' any cha-cha with one of my clients. You got that?"

His mustache twitched from side to side like the tail of an annoyed cat as he glared down at his dirty wingtips. "Mmmbrl."

"What kind of answer is that?" Giselle demanded. "Mmmbrl? I want you to promise me, Remy Doucet. I want your solemn oath that you will *not* embarrass me."

Remy rubbed a hand across his jaw. The devil on his shoulder told him there was a lot of leeway in the interpretation of that statement. He grinned up at his sister. "I promise."

Annick rolled her dark eyes and laughed in disbelief. "That's like askin' *m'sieu renard* to stay outa the henhouse and believin' him when he says *mais* yeah."

Remy shot her a look. "Who asked you, *gosse*?"

"Nobody. And don't you call me a brat."

"Brat."

She stuck her tongue out at him. Remy grinned and mussed his baby sister's short hair. Annick might have been twenty-three with a promising career in law ahead of her, but he still enjoyed teasing her as much as he had when she'd been thirteen.

Giselle shook her head and sighed a long-suffering sigh. "Ah, me, who would guess by the way you two act you're a future lawyer and a man with a college education?"

"The Amazing Kreskin?" Remy offered with a hopeful look.

Giving in to his boyish charm, Giselle chuckled. "Oh, Remy, what am I gonna do with you?"

"Dance!" He hopped off the desk, grabbed his sister, and swung her into a two-step.

"Oooh, my poor old aching back!" Alistair Urquhart-Butler groaned. His face screwed up in a grimace, he cracked one eye open ever so slightly to see how Danielle was reacting. Oblivious to the performance, Danielle moved around the bed straightening his covers, her lovely mouth frowning, worry lining her forehead. "I'm so sorry I'm of no help to you, lass. How are you getting on with the wee bairns, then? Fine, I trust."

"Oh, just peachy," Danielle drawled. She poured him a glass of ice water and handed him the brown bottle of pills he kept on hand for his bad back. She watched as Butler shook two out and tossed them back, making a great show of swallowing them down.

He sighed and shook his head and looked generally woebegone. "I feel terrible being brought down in the line of duty this way with you trusting me to help you with the children—"

"It wasn't your fault," Danielle said, sitting down on the edge of the bed beside the man who had helped raise her off and on during her formative years.

Butler was as much a father to her and the other Hamilton offspring as Laird Hamilton himself was. Stern, but loving, he had always been there when one of them needed a helping hand or a smack on the fanny. He loved them all like family, she knew, and his feelings were reciprocated.

She studied him now as he leaned back against the carved headboard in his Hamilton tartan pajamas with the clan crest embroidered on the pocket, thinking he never looked any different to her. No matter how long she was away she knew when she came back Butler would be the same man who'd patched up her skinned knees and scolded her for getting sick on her father's cigars. He was past sixty, but he still had his full head of fine red hair, which he had always worn neatly combed and parted on the right, held in place with witch hazel gel. He had the same bold Scottish features as her father—the high, broad forehead, the stubborn chin and substantial nose—and the same undiluted burr even though both of them had lived in the States for more than half their lives.

"Still, I wasna counting on this atall," he said, making another pained face and checking to see that she'd caught it this time.

Danielle pleated the plaid bedspread with her fingers and frowned. "Divide and conquer. That's their strategy. But I don't want you to worry about it. You lie here and rest. I'll manage."

"See there, lass, I told you you could handle this," Butler said with pride. He started to sit up, thought better of it, and leaned gingerly back against the pillows, wincing. "I knew if you but put your fears behind you—"

"I've hired a nanny," Danielle said, as much to stem the flow of Butler's pep talk as to impart the good news. She hadn't put her fears behind her. She didn't think she could stand having him praise her for rising above her past when she doubted she would ever be able to do that. The memory of what she'd done would always be too fresh in her mind, the pain too deep in her heart.

Butler's keen blue eyes widened a fraction. His voice lost all trace of weary suffering. He looked a bit peeved. "You've done what?"

"I've done what every good rich girl does in the face of adversity—I've hired help." She rose and straightened her fresh melon-colored tank top, then double-checked the baby monitor hanging from her belt to make sure it was working. "He seems perfectly competent, if a bit unconventional—"

"He?"

"Remy Doucet. He'll be moving in tonight. I'm sure he'll do fine. Don't you worry about a thing. I'd better go check on the baby now," she said, fussing with the monitor. "Have you got everything you need?"

"Aye," he said absently.

Danielle glanced around the room. It wasn't as large as the one she had commandeered upstairs, but it was certainly comfortable. Besides the carved mahogany double bed there was the marble-topped nightstand, a matching dresser, and a tall armoire that housed a television with a VCR and a stereo. Butler's quarters had all the comforts of home and the added benefit of being off-limits to the Beauvais children. Danielle would gladly have traded places with him—bad back and all.

"Get some rest," she said, moving toward the door.

"Aye, you too now, lass," he mumbled.

If she hadn't been so preoccupied with her own thoughts, Danielle might have noticed that he sounded just a little bit guilty. But she was too tired and too flustered and too determined to do her duty until her replacement arrived. She slipped out the door of Butler's room and headed up the servant's staircase. All she had to do was hang in there until Remy arrived, then she would steer clear of him and the Beauvais darlings. They could keep each other occupied for the next three weeks and Suzannah could take her idea of family influence and choke on it.

Butler held his breath as he listened to Danielle's footsteps fade away. The poor lass. She looked like death warmed over. He'd been so sure she would rise to the occasion, but the purple crescents under her eyes told a different tale. Now she'd gone and hired a nanny. Things were not going according to plan.

Shaking his head, he tossed the covers back and pushed himself out of bed. He put the two pills he had palmed back in their bottle, sure that Danielle was in too dazed a state to notice the supply wasn't dwindling. He stretched both hands toward the high ceiling then bent and touched his toes. When he had all the kinks out, he reached for the phone on the nightstand and punched out a number.

"It's me," he said in a low voice. "We've got a wee bit of a problem."

# Four

"What's that, Auntie Dan-L?" Ambrose asked as he peered through his Lone Ranger mask at the casserole.

"Macaroni surprise."

"What's the surprise?"

Jeremy gave a derisive snort as he poked at the noodles with a long-handled spoon. "If we eat it and live, she'll be surprised."

"Not to mention disappointed," Danielle muttered under her breath, leveling a glare at Jeremy.

The children had caught on rather quickly to the fact that she was not a cook. She knew she was not a cook; the news came as no surprise to her. The sense of hurt did, however. She had gone to the effort to make the kids a home-cooked meal, hoping that would in some way make them look at her as a kind of mother figure.

*Face it, Danielle,* she told herself, swallowing down the bitter taste of defeat, *you can't bond successfully through macaroni. You can't bond successfully, period. Who are you trying to fool?*

She had known for some time that she wasn't cut out for this. So why was the idea choking her up now, she wondered, as she stared morosely at the unappetizing casserole. She liked her life the way it was. She was free to travel wherever she wanted, whenever she wanted. If she got the itch to snap a few pictures of the Mayan ruins at Chichen Itza, all she had to do was pack up her cameras and go. If she wanted to spend the entire night working on printing techniques in her darkroom, there was no one to complain to her about being neglected.

Her life was unencumbered by people who needed to know where she was every waking minute or wanted to make demands on her time. Her relationships with men never lasted, so there was minimal distraction there. She was basically free to pour herself completely into her art and that was the way she wanted it.

She would always be an artist first. And as an artist she required a spare, focused life. The muse was a selfish mistress, demanding all the artist's attention, a shameless wanton who pushed away all others vying for the artist's time. It was because of her muse Danielle didn't know how to cook anything more edible than limp macaroni. But an artist was all she had ever wanted to be.

She'd spent less than a week with the Beauvais kids and already she'd had a stomach full of the family scene. The constant tension, the constant distractions were overwhelming her. Danielle Hamilton didn't need a family. No sirree. What she needed right now was a ticket out of this funhouse. She missed her peace and quiet . . . sort of.

"Do we have to eat this?" Tinks asked, staring at the steaming lump of gook on her plate. "It's gross."

Danielle scowled at her and swore to herself that her feelings weren't hurt. Her shoulders slumped as she stared down at the disgusting mess on her plate. They were right. It was gross.

"It looks like cooked brains," Jeremy said with malicious delight as he reached his fork onto Dahlia's plate and stirred her dinner around. "Gooey, slimy cooked possum brains."

Dahlia looked up in horror, her freckles standing out in sharp relief against her white face. "Make him stop it! Make him stop, Aunt Danielle! I'm gonna gag!"

Jeremy chortled maniacally, his pleasure in grossing out his sister such that he could barely keep himself on his chair. "Gooey gator brains! Slippery, slimy snake innards!"

"I'm gonna throw up!" Dahlia cried.

Danielle gave her nephew her sternest look. It didn't faze him. "Jeremy, stop it or you won't get any supper."

He rolled his eyes. "*That's* a threat? Ha!"

"Look, guys," Danielle said, diplomatically taking another tack. "This stuff is good for you. It's loaded with protein."

"So are cockroaches," Jeremy muttered. "We don't eat them."

"It could be arranged." There was just enough menace in Danielle's voice to give credence to her words. Four red-haired heads bent over their plates. Forks clicked against china.

Danielle ignored her own plate on the excuse that she had to feed Eudora, who sat beside her in her yellow high chair. Knowing nothing about baby diets, she had decided it would be potluck night. She had chosen three jars of strained and mushed stuff on the basis of a pleasing color combination. Eudora didn't seem to mind. She ate every other spoonful with the relish of a gourmand and spat alternating helpings at Danielle.

Unaffected, Danielle went on feeding the baby.

Getting spat on was nothing. She'd been spat on by a cobra in Africa and still had gotten the shot she wanted. It was one of her most famous wildlife photos and had graced the cover of the *National Geographic*. She could handle getting spat on. It was the least of the abuse she'd taken so far from Suzannah's little ghouls.

Eudora grabbed a handful of peach cobbler and flung it into Danielle's face with an exuberant cry of "Whee!"

Danielle gritted her teeth, wondering how long it was going to take for her to grind the enamel right off them. Lord, she couldn't wait for Remy to relieve her.

Relief? Was that what she called getting kissed until her ears rang? Her toes tingled at the memory. Brother, that man knew how to kiss! But that was irrelevant, she told herself sternly, spooning up another glob of pureed peas on the baby's rubber-covered spoon. Remy's kiss might have been a doozie, but it was in the past, over, finished. From this moment on she was going to endeavor to behave like the mature woman she was. No more losing her head over young, brawny, devastatingly sexy Cajun men. No more sizzler kisses. No more clinches in the nursery. No more fantasizing about his fabulous fanny.

She stared up at a spot of pulverized peas dotting the kitchen wall, fanning her flushed face with her free hand. Well, maybe it wouldn't hurt to fantasize a teensy bit. After all, at her age, fantasizing about a younger man was probably *all* she was ever going to do. And if she were to pick a man's fanny to fantasize about, Remy Doucet's was it. The man had a real power tush.

But no touching, she told herself, frowning. Absolutely, positively *no* touching.

Lord, she groaned, her fingers were itching to touch him! She'd probably go crazy and grope him the minute they were alone in the same room. What lousy timing. She'd never met a man she wanted to grope more than Remy Doucet and he was off-limits. Even if she hadn't just hired him as a nanny, there was the little matter of the fact that he hadn't even been a twinkle in Papa Doucet's eye when she was discovering the wonders of grammar school.

"My luck," she muttered, her arm swinging back and forth as she tried to zero in on Eudora's dodging mouth.

Well, she would just have to leash her lust before he arrived.

"Hey, Danielle," a melodic male voice called cheerfully from the kitchen doorway. "Where you at?"

As all her insides turned into curlicues at the sight of Remy in snug jeans and a black polo shirt, Danielle forced her mind to ponder his typical New Orleans greeting. Why didn't he ask *how* she was? He knew *where* she was. She was sitting right there in front of him with mushed gook all over her. Decidedly unromantic, she thought, glancing down at the front of her blouse, which had been tie-dyed with Gerber's finest.

A little tingle of panic shot through her. She didn't want romantic, couldn't have romantic. Nothing about this arrangement was romantic. He was the kids' nanny. She had to think of him as Mary Poppins with five o'clock shadow.

"Hello, Mr. Doucet," she said, offering him a businesslike smile. "Kids, say hello to Mr. Doucet."

When no sound issued forth except Eudora's happy beet-juicy gurgle, Danielle glanced around the table. The kids had jumped ship. She had been so immersed in her thoughts about Remy's masculine attributes, she hadn't even noticed them leave. Yet another example of what a fine mother she would make.

"They're in watchin' TV," he said, setting down a

maroon nylon carryall. He settled his big hands at his waist and grimaced at the congealing lump of macaroni on an abandoned dinner plate, the corners of his mustache tugging down around his mouth.

"Go ahead. Say it," Danielle snapped defensively. "I can take it. It's written all over your face. I'm a lousy cook."

"You're a lousy cook." Cautiously he poked at the mess with a fork, as if he expected it to come to life and attack him. "What is it?"

"Macaroni surprise."

"Did they eat it?"

"No."

"I'm not surprised."

He was a little disappointed, though. He would never have admitted it, but he was a chauvinist through and through. Where he came from, women knew how to cook—actually, most everybody knew how to cook. They also knew how to raise children. Danielle didn't appear to be adept at either of those womanly arts.

She sure was pretty, though. That made up for a lot, he thought, taking in her perfect patrician features as she glared up at him defiantly. Her translucent gray eyes glittered like sterling. Her chin jutted forward aggressively. How she managed to look so dignified while covered with baby food was beyond him. He decided it was the mark of a true lady.

"You see this finger?" she asked, raising her left fist with the forefinger extended. "This is my cooking finger."

"Your cooking finger?"

"This finger can dial the number of every major take-out place in every city in the world. I ask you, what more do I need?"

Remy picked a striped dish towel off the corner of the table and swiped a speck of peach cobbler off the tip of her nose. "A shower."

Danielle blinked. Even through terry cloth his touch was electric. Prince Abdul Rifal of Dakjir had once taken a fingertip tour of her face through a silken veil and it hadn't affected her nearly as profoundly. Forcing the thought away, she looked down at the front of her T-shirt. Sunburst patterns in green, ruby, and peach were splashed across her chest in lumpy, liquidy glory. The same colors dotted her arms like three-dimensional freckles.

"Yuk."

Remy clicked his tongue and shook his dark head. "You're a mess, you are, *chère*. Mebbe we oughta just take you out back and hose you down."

"No thanks. I like the idea of a hot shower much better."

"Me too," he said in that intimate, velvety tone of voice that just reeked of sin. He bent over her, one hand on the table, one on the back of her chair. His eyes captured hers like hot black magnets capturing steel. He waggled his brows. "You need any help with that, *chère*?"

The mere thought made Danielle's insides go as soft as the overcooked macaroni on her plate. The picture of the two of them in the shower stall together, steam rising, soap bubbles sliding over slick skin, darn near made her faint.

"No!" she said suddenly, leaning back in her chair, trying to escape his male aura. "I can manage."

"You sure?" Remy murmured, forgetting what little sense of propriety he had as he stared at Danielle's breasts as they thrust up toward him. They were small but firm and round and unfettered by the bonds of a bra. "I'm real good with my hands."

Danielle's breath soughed through her parted lips. She could imagine the feel of those big hands stroking her, caressing her, cupping her breast and guiding it to his mouth as the shower pounded down on them. Her gaze fastened helplessly on Remy's mouth, so close, so tempting. He leaned a little nearer.

"What happened to your pledge of good behavior?" she asked breathlessly, clinging to the last ragged threads of her sanity.

His eyes sparkled as he gave her his slow piratelike smile. His smoky voice stroked over her like a caress. "This is as good as it gets."

"Oh, my . . ."

Eudora gave a sudden squeal of delight and mushed a handful of peas into Remy's face. "Eii-up, da da da da!" she chortled merrily, clapping her hands together and splashing vegetable matter in all directions, effectively breaking the mood, much to Danielle's relief—or was it dismay?

"Looks like I'm gonna have to join you in that shower now, yes?" Remy said to Danielle with a grin as he scraped the bilious green goo off his face with the dish towel.

"No, I don't think so." Danielle ducked under his arm and rose to her full height, eliminating his advantage. She composed herself admirably just long enough to tell him where to put his things, then she dashed for the door, chanting "no touching, no touching" under her breath like an incantation against evil spirits.

Remy straightened and watched her flee, guilt poking at him as he thought of his promise to his sister.

Eudora squealed and reached her arms up, begging to be taken out of her high chair. She looked like she'd been to a body-painting salon. Her little fingers were dripping baby food. The front of her romper was covered. Peach cobbler had been run through her duck fuzz hair like gel, spiking it up in a punk fashion. Her face was coated with pureed peas. She looked enormously happy, though, in spite of, or maybe because of, her slovenly state.

"Happy as a pig in pink mud, aren't you?" Remy said with a chuckle. Heedless of his shirt, he scooped her up in his arms and headed for the door. "Come on, *pichouette*, looks like you're the only lady I get to bathe tonight."

By the time Danielle emerged from her room, freshly showered and dressed in trendy loose purple cotton slacks and a matching top, Remy had bathed Eudora and dressed her for bed in a snowy white sleeper with a herd of hopping yellow bunnies printed on it. The older children were still firmly entrenched in front of the television, absorbed in the latest escapade of *McGyver*.

"They're actually quiet," Danielle murmured, looking in at them from the hall. Under the chilling spray of the showerhead she had wrestled her rampant hormones into submission and righted her normal calm sense of self. Her unsettled emotions had crawled back under the carpet of wry humor. She felt in control of herself again, and reasonably certain she would stay that way—just as long as she didn't come within kissing distance of Remy again. She checked the distance between them and sent him a sardonic smile. "If I didn't know better, I might mistake them for a normal family."

"Aw, come on, sugar." Remy chuckled, conveniently forgetting the afternoon episode on the roof. He lowered Eudora into the playpen that sat just inside the family room door and handed her a foam ball which she promptly began to chew on. Straightening, he settled his hands at the waistband of his jeans. "This household isn't so different from any other house with kids in it."

"I'd call that one heck of an argument for planned parenthood," Danielle quipped. She took a step back from the domestic scene and nodded toward the back of the house. "If you have a minute, I'll introduce you to Butler now. It's time for his pain medication. Maybe if we're lucky he'll share some with us."

Remy frowned at that, but decided she was joking. He fell into step behind her, admiring the sway of her hips. "Who is this Butler fella? You mentioned him this afternoon, but what with all that cryin' and carryin' on I forgot to ask."

Danielle shot him a look that told him she didn't appreciate the reminder of her disgrace. "Butler is the butler."

Stunned to a standstill, Remy gave a snort of outrage. "Well, call the poor man by his name, at least! The days of the name going with the station are long gone, even down here. And if you think for a minute I'm gonna let you get away with callin' me Nanny, you can just think again," he said, jabbing the air with his forefinger.

Danielle pushed his hand aside and rolled her eyes. "Save your temper for a better day, *Mr. Doucet*. Butler *is* his name—Alistair Urquhart-Butler."

A deep flush seeped under Remy's tan. "Oh."

"Oh." Danielle shook her head. "Jeeze, what do you take me for?"

A rich, spoiled, pampered woman who paid servants to do every job she deemed unpleasant. But he didn't say that in view of the fact that she could fire him just as easily as she had hired him, and he needed—no, *wanted* this job. He wanted the chance to find out what other misconceptions he had about Danielle.

"I guess I'm not all that familiar with the way wealthy people treat their hired help," he admitted.

Danielle stopped at Butler's door and gave Remy a strange look. "I would have thought you'd be well acquainted with the relationship. Mr. and Mrs. Factory Worker don't hire many nannies. Who have you been working for?"

"Oooohhh . . ." Remy's throat constricted around his answer and he was about to choke on it when a wavering voice called out on the other side of the door.

"Danni? Is that you, lass?"

Danielle swung the door open and strode across the room with a concerned look on her face. "You sound terrible! Are you feeling worse?"

Butler shifted positions against the pillows, wincing but putting on a brave face for Danielle. "Oh, dinna fash yourself, lass. The pain is terrible, but I can bear it. 'Tis the worry that's about to do me in."

"I told you not to worry. I've got everything under control. I've brought the new nanny in to meet you."

Butler raised a brow in surprise as Remy stepped forward, his broad shoulders nearly filling the doorway.

"This is Remy Doucet," Danielle said, stepping aside to fuss with Butler's pill bottle as the men regarded one another. "Remy, this is Alistair Urquhart-Butler, devoted retainer of the Hamilton clan for lo these many years."

The men shook hands, Remy raising a brow at the strength of the older man's grip. Butler quickly let go and groaned a little as he settled back against his mountain of pillows. "I'd get up, Mr. Do-sit, but as you can see, I'm incapacitated."

"Much to my dismay," Danielle said. "Butler was going to look after the children. I was just brought in for window dressing."

"Well, there's no need for you to worry yourself, Mr. Butler," Remy said with a deceptively placid smile. "I'll take real good care of the kids." His voice dropped a husky fraction of a note. "And Miss Danielle too."

He delivered his little addendum with a perfect poker face and still Danielle blushed. Immediately she felt Butler's keen blue eyes dart to her face, homing in like heat-seeking missiles. It was as bad as when she'd been fourteen, spending the summer at her father's home, and Butler had somehow known just by looking at her that she was engaging in nightly necking sessions with Jamey Sheridan from across the lake. He looked at her now and she was certain he could see every hormone she had gravitating toward Remy Doucet.

She thrust his pills at him. "Mr. Doucet comes from one of the best agencies in the city."

"Does he now?" Butler never took his eyes from his mistress's flaming face. Danielle squirmed and looked away, missing completely the act of Butler palming his medication. When he handed the bottle back to her, she gladly took it for something to hang on to. "And just how long have you been a nanny, Mr. Do-sit?"

Remy cleared his throat and handed the supine butler a glass of water from the nightstand. His dark eyes caught Butler's and held them with a meaningful look. "Better wash those big horse pills down, Mr. Butler. We wouldn't want you to choke now. Those pain killers are so big, a man might as well just leave 'em in his fist and swallow that too."

Butler blanched and coughed a bit in genuine distress. Taking a sip from the glass of water, he forced a wan smile. "What a relief it is to know Danielle will have help with the children."

A wry smile twitched up one corner of Remy's mustache. "Isn't it, though?"

"How was your dinner?" Danielle asked, suspiciously eyeing the empty plate on the bed tray.

"Fine, lass." Butler twitched the bedspread to make sure the portion nearest the floor covered the waste-basket full of macaroni surprise. He sat up a little straighter and stretched his arms a bit. "About the meals. You know, I'm fair certain I'll feel up to standing a wee bit tomorrow. Perhaps I could resume my duties in the kitchen."

"Absolutely not!"

"I can handle it, Mr. Butler." Remy grinned. "I'm a good cook . . . for a price."

"Name it," Butler blurted out.

"Hey!" Danielle propped her hands on her hips and scowled at the pair of them.

Butler gave her an apologetic look. "No offense, lass, but Julia Child you're not."

"Oh, fine," she snapped, unreasonably hurt at having her paltry domestic skills criticized. "I'll gladly turn my apron over to the Cookin' Cajun here. Everybody knows I wasn't cut out for kitchen duty or diaper detail."

Remy gave her a curious look, having picked up a little too keenly the bitterness in her tone. He glanced from her to Butler and back, reading a tense mix of emotions on the two faces.

"Now, lass—"

"We ought to let you rest, Butler," Danielle said stiffly, fearing she had already let something slip that she would rather have kept firmly tucked away. She didn't like the way Remy was looking at her and she knew she didn't want to hear what Butler was about to say. She backed toward the door, fighting the need to simply turn and hightail it. "Besides, we really shouldn't cluster ourselves all in one room this way. Jeremy is liable to nail the door shut."

Remy bid Butler a restful night and followed Danielle back out into the hall. "You sure you don't mind me cookin', *chère*?"

"Mind? Why should I mind?" She flapped her arms in an exaggerated shrug and twirled around the kitchen like a demented ballet dancer, gesturing to the stove, the cupboards, the gourmet gadgets lining the countertops. "Cook! Cook away! Cook yourself into a frenzy!"

"You just seem a little upset, is all," he observed, taking a baby bottle from the drainer by the sink. He went to the refrigerator, took out a carton of milk and filled the bottle, keeping one watchful eye on Danielle throughout the entire process.

The lady was rattled about something and he was willing to bet it was something a lot more important than macaroni surprise. There were things going on here he knew nothing about, but he could feel the undercurrents just the same. He could also feel the need to reach out to Danielle, to offer support and comfort. It unnerved him a little bit. She wasn't the kind of woman who normally inspired protective feelings in him, not by a long shot.

Danielle watched him shut the refrigerator with a breath-catching little bump of his hip. He went to the stove and set about warming the baby's bottle, his movements as sure as if he'd done this every day of his life. For the short time she'd been in charge of Eudora she had gone around with a book on child care in one hand until she'd practically had to have the thing surgically removed.

"I seem upset to you?" she asked. All the reminders of her ineptitude ganged up on her at once and lodged like a rock in her chest. The calm she had worked so hard to resurrect had deserted her utterly, leaving her feeling more unsettled than ever. "Well, in addition to being a rotten cook and a lousy baby-sitter, I'm also a temperamental bitch," she said, her voice hoarse from trying to hold back her true emotions. She tossed her hair back over her shoulder and gave Remy her haughtiest look, though she wouldn't meet his eyes. "Us rich women are often like that, you know. You might as well get used to it."

With that she flounced from the room, leaving nothing behind but the sting of her words and a fragrant trail of Giorgio.

Remy made a face and whistled through his teeth as he stared at the swinging door. "The lady bites like a gator. I wonder why."

# *Five*

Feeling like a fool, Danielle wandered barefoot out onto the wide veranda that graced the front of the Beauvais house. Remy had to believe she was a little unhinged after her performance in the kitchen. She was beginning to wonder about it herself.

The time she'd spent in Tibet had been intended as healing time, time to put things in perspective, time to reconcile herself to her future and dull the memory of what had happened in London. She had spent months living in a simple shanty on the edge of the Chang Tang plateau with only a yak and a goat for company. Her days had consisted of work, shooting endless rolls of film of the bleak Tibetan landscape. Her nights had consisted of quiet meditation. She had returned feeling at peace with herself. But that sense of peace had been both false and fragile. Now she felt a fool for ever having believed in it.

As a sense of despair welled up inside her, she hugged a smooth wooden column, pressed her cheek against the white painted wood. She was vaguely aware of the heavy scent of flowers in the thick warm air, sweet and cloying like a bordello madam's perfume on a Saturday night. The sun had set but darkness had yet to wrap its cloak around the Big Easy. The Garden District was quiet. The French Quarter would just be coming to life.

Out on the street a carriage full of tourists clomped past, drawn by a tired-looking black horse. The tourists craned their necks to get a look at the magnificent homes that lined the block. Cameras swiveled in Danielle's direction and she managed to smile at the irony of her being a subject of a photographer's curiosity.

Remy stepped out onto the veranda with Eudora tucked into the crook of one brawny arm, an unlit cigarette dangling from his lips. Danielle watched from the corner of her eye as he settled himself back in one corner of the porch swing and gave the baby her bottle. His dark eyes drifted her way and studied her openly for a long moment before he spoke.

"Why don't you sit down, *chère*?" he asked, his voice low, his tone not overtly sexual, but inviting and compelling.

Danielle felt as if she were walking through ankle-deep molasses as she crossed the porch. Her instincts were screaming at her to run away, but she blatantly ignored them. She was a grown woman, a woman of the world, a—how she was growing to hate this word—mature woman. She would sit on this swing and have a civil conversation with this man, just as she would get through these next weeks living in the same house with him.

She wedged herself into the opposite corner of the swing, drew her feet up to the seat, and wrapped her arms around her knees. "I'm sorry I snapped at you in the kitchen. I've been a little on edge lately."

Remy continued to study her, unblinking, his expression closed. "Why is that?"

There was a wealth of reasons, none of which she

was willing to explain to him. The temptation, however, was strong. She felt a part of herself wanting to tell him, and that kind of wanting was a dangerous thing when having was out of the question.

"I'm not used to being around so many people," she said. It was at least part of the truth. "The part of Tibet I stayed in isn't exactly Times Square."

Remy took his cigarette from his lips and tucked it behind his ear like a pencil. His thick brows drew together as he looked at her with open curiosity. "What were you doing all that time in such a place?"

Hurting, thinking, doing penance, and trying to heal, she thought, but she glanced away from him again before he could see any of those answers in her eyes. "I was taking pictures. I'm a photographer."

"Oh yeah? Like for a magazine or what?"

"I sometimes contribute photographs to magazines. Most of my work ends in galleries and books. My series from Tibet will be a book. *Moonscapes, Landscapes: A Portrait of Tibet.*"

Remy looked suitably impressed. There was something else in his expression, too, though, something like concern. He shifted Eudora in his arms, adjusted the angle of her bottle, scooted over on the bench an inch or so. "You travel around a lot doing that?"

"All over the world."

"And it doesn't bother you?"

"Why would it bother me? I grew up living out of suitcases. My mother was an international model. She took me with her everywhere she went."

"But don't you ever get the urge to just stay home, put down roots, raise a family?"

"My home is wherever I hang my camera bag."

"And the rest?"

"Is none of your business, Mr. Doucet," she said coolly, lifting her slim patrician nose a notch.

Remy scowled at her tone of voice. She was trying to make him back off. He didn't for a minute believe she was the kind of society lady who demanded the hired help bob and tug their forelocks in her presence. That was the impression she was trying to give him now, though.

She had unfolded her long legs from the seat of the swing and demurely crossed them in that impossible pretzel-twist taught at finishing schools. She was good at looking cool and unapproachable, but the act was wasted on him. He had held her, had felt the fragile vulnerability that lay beneath her surface; he had tasted the sweetness in her kiss. There was much more to Danielle Hamilton than prim deportment and a taste for the finer things, and he had every intention of uncovering the secrets that lingered in her big eyes.

"You like all that traveling?" he asked, unable to keep the amazement out of his voice. He inched a little closer to her.

Danielle relaxed a degree as he let go of the topics she dreaded most. She settled back into the flowered cushions of the swing again and nodded. "I love discovering different parts of the world, what the people are like, what the food is like, the environment, the history. It's all fascinating to me."

Remy looked down at Eudora, frowning absently. He couldn't understand that kind of wanderlust. It made him vaguely uncomfortable to think of it and to think that Danielle was so different from him. He would have preferred their only major differences to be the fun kind—anatomical.

Danielle studied him as he seemed to lose himself in thought. A sweet pang shot through her chest at the sight of little Eudora snuggling against Remy's chest, her fair lashes fluttering against her chubby cheeks like fairy's wings as she drifted into sleep. She looked completely relaxed, as if she felt absolutely safe and secure, and Remy looked oddly natural with the baby in his arms. It didn't make sense. A big, brawny guy like Remy Doucet, who seemed to exude masculinity from every inch of his brawny body, shouldn't have been so at ease feeding a baby. But he held Eudora with the kind of second-nature casualness that came from long experience.

Danielle caught herself wishing she could trade places with her neice. She had a feeling nuzzling against Remy's chest would be a very cozy place to fall asleep . . . or something. The memory of his arms around her came back with the tempting lure of a siren's call. She had to struggle to remember that the siren's victims always met with disaster—which was what she was headed for fantasizing about Remy's chest.

She cleared her mind of romantic notions and cleared her throat to break the languid mood that had settled over them as tangibly as the Louisiana humidity. "I take it you've been here all your life."

"Pretty much. My family's been living on the Bayou Noir for 'bout two hundred years."

"Gee, you don't look a day over a hundred and three," she said dryly.

Remy smiled like a crocodile, his dark eyes glittering as he leaned a little closer. "Does that mean you don't still think I'm too young for you, sugar?"

Danielle snapped her teeth together and fumed while her cheeks flushed a shade to rival the geraniums that spilled out of stone pots on either side of the front door.

Not wanting to scare her off, Remy changed the subject before she could say anything. "I moved from Lou'siana once. I was working for an oil company and had to transfer to Scotland—the outer Hebrides." He rolled his eyes and shuddered at the memory.

Danielle had spent a month in the Hebrides one summer. It was a harsh place, but beautiful. She had enjoyed the sounds of the wind and the sea, the rugged treeless landscape, the earthy practicality and hospitality of the islanders. Remy obviously had not.

"I had to come back home," he said. "This is where my family is. How could I live someplace else?"

Danielle shrugged. "My family is scattered all over the globe. That doesn't makes us less of a family."

"How many brothers and sisters do you have?"

"Five. We're all related only through our father, though, except Drew and Tony—they're twins."

"*Bon dieu!* Your papa, he's really had *five* wives?"

She nodded and shrugged, her angular shoulders lifting and falling gracefully. "The Hamilton curse," she said blandly. "Women fall in love with Laird at first sight. They just can't stand being married to him. Oddly enough, they've all remained friends after the divorces. It's not at all uncommon for one or more of the exes to be in residence at the compound at any given time."

"And you believe in this curse, *chère*?"

Danielle wasn't sure how much credence she put in the curse, but she certainly couldn't dispute the fact that her relationships with men didn't last. When she was feeling practical she admitted she wasn't an easy person to live with. When she was feeling put upon she blamed the curse. "Well, I'm not exactly a missus now, am I?" she said by way of an answer.

"Mrs. Beauvais is."

"Suzannah is the exception to the rule."

Danielle looked past him, through the window into the house. From her position she couldn't see the children, but the television was still glowing and mumbling.

"What did you do to the Wild Bunch?" she asked dryly. "They haven't been this quiet since they were in their mother's womb."

"I told 'em I learned how to be a nanny through a correspondence course while I was in prison."

Danielle's heart froze for one terrifying second,

then lurched into overdrive. What had she done now? She should have insisted on checking his references. She had been too enthralled with his fabulous fanny to think that he might have been a psychotic killer or something. For a split second she thought of snatching the baby from his arms and dashing into the house, but she dismissed the idea. She would rather take her chances with an escaped convict than be locked inside the same house with Jeremy Beauvais.

"Relax, darlin'," Remy said on a chuckle. "I'm just exactly what I appear to be."

No great comfort there, Danielle decided. He appeared to be deliciously, intoxicatingly, irresistibly male. He appeared to be the answer to every erotic dream she'd ever had. He appeared to be too young for them to be included in the same demographic group. She swallowed hard and barred her teeth in a parody of a smile. "Wonderful."

"I think you're pretty terrific, too, Danielle."

Danielle felt everything inside her begin to overheat. It was then that she realized Remy was no longer safely tucked back into his own corner of the swing. His muscular thigh was brushing against hers. He had slid his left arm along the back of the bench so that his fingertips were resting just behind her bare shoulder. He leaned a little closer. She gave him a dour look that made him sit up but didn't quell him into retreating to his own side of the swing.

"Can't blame a guy for tryin', now can you?" he said, giving her his innocent altar boy look.

"You're a regular Cajun Casanova, aren't you?" Danielle accused. "And with a baby in your arms. You ought to be ashamed."

He didn't look ashamed, but he did glance down at Eudora dozing contentedly on his arm. A soft, heart-stealing smile lifted the corners of his mustache. "She's a little doll, *oui*?"

"Yes, she is," Danielle murmured, biting her lip as she looked at her little niece. Eudora was unquestionably precious with her pudgy cheeks and duckling fuzz hair. No one would have guessed from looking at her she was going to grow up to be one of the infamous Beauvais clan. She had stolen Danielle's heart immediately and now that heart squeezed a little in her chest as Danielle reached out a slightly trembling hand to brush at the baby's fine red hair. "I think she even likes me some of the time."

The wistfulness in her voice hit Remy square in the chest. He looked at her now when her guard was completely down and a knot of some unidentifiable emotion wedged itself into his throat. The woman who had the ability to look fierce and imperious and as icy as a winter day in the Hebrides now looked haunted and insecure and filled with longing.

"Sure, she likes you," he whispered, brushing back a lock of Danielle's angel hair with his free hand. "You wanna hold her?"

Danielle made a face. "I'm not very good at that."

"Don't say that," he said in that soft seductive tone that never failed to make Danielle's toes curl. "All you need is a little practice."

He scooted closer to her again, until his thigh was solidly pressed to hers. Danielle felt the heat of him and wondered if it was possible for flesh to fuse through a layer of denim and cotton gauze.

"Here," he said, positioning the baby to slide her into Danielle's arms. "All you gotta do is relax, dar-lin'."

With his dark eyes locked on hers, Danielle completely lost track of the conversation. The moment was suddenly charged with all kinds of possibilities—possibilities that involved a lot less clothing than she was wearing now. As her breath grew painfully short, her nipples hardened beneath the suddenly abrasive fabric of her tank top. Memories of the kiss she'd shared with Remy flooded her foggy head—the brush and tickle of his mustache against her skin, the sensuous fullness of his firm lower lip, the clean earthy scent of him. She was on the verge of begging him to kiss her again when Eudora's weight settled into her arms.

She looked down at the sleeping child and automatically tightened her hold. Eudora squirmed and made a face in her sleep.

"Relax," Remy coaxed gently. "Don't squeeze her; she's not an accordion. That's right. Just relax, *chère*, she won't break."

He slid his arm directly around Danielle's shoulders this time, not bothering with subterfuge. She needed his support now. The sight of her holding the baby, her gray eyes full of uncertainty, stirred feelings deep within him—protective feelings, primitive feelings. There was a tenderness, a sweet, aching kind of tenderness that shamed the mere lust he'd felt for her earlier.

"*Bien*," he murmured, leaning down to brush his lips against her temple. "That's fine. You're doing just fine."

Danielle soaked up his words like a dry sponge absorbing rain. In that instant she didn't feel forty, she felt afraid. And Remy wasn't too young, he was too good, too sweet. She lifted her gaze, intending to dispel the magic with a wry remark, but her heart caught in her throat as she met his earnest, caring look.

Remy stroked his fingertips down her cheek, his thumb brushing the corner of her mouth. Then before the spell could be broken, he leaned down and caught her parted lips with his. It was a sweet kiss, a soft kiss, not threatening or demanding. It was all too brief, and yet it was long enough to send all of Danielle's senses into a frenzy.

She could have put it down to the fact that she

hadn't been near a man in a long time. Or she could have put it down to the stress she'd been under recently. But under all the excuses lay the basic truth—she was attracted to this man in a way she couldn't remember ever having been attracted before. It was frightening, particularly now when she had decided she wasn't going to find fireworks or bliss, now when she had finally resigned herself to the fact that some dreams weren't meant to come true.

Looking down at Eudora, she tried to clear some of the huskiness from her voice, but managed only a hoarse whisper when she said, "Maybe you should take her up to bed now."

Remy sat back thinking it was Danielle he wanted to take to bed. He wanted to hold her and love away all the shadows in her pretty gray eyes. He wanted to kiss her and bury himself inside her and tell her how pretty she was and how hot she made him. *Bon Dieu,* he thought, it was a wonder the swing didn't burn away beneath him.

A brief flash of movement at the front door caught his attention and he glanced over expecting to see one of the children, but the figure that quickly ducked back was much too tall to be a Beauvais. He rubbed the back of his neck and narrowed his eyes in thought as he pulled his cigarette out from behind his ear and planted it in the corner of his mouth. There was something very strange going on around here.

"That Butler," he began. "What sort of fella is he?"

"Butler?" Danielle repeated dumbly, her brain still shorting out.

"Yeah. He wouldn't—"

His question was cut short by the resounding *Ka-boom!* of an explosion taking place somewhere inside the house.

Remy bolted to his feet and dashed for the door. Danielle stood and stumbled as the swing hit her in the back of the knees. She snatched Eudora tightly up against her shoulder, waking the baby and scaring her so that she immediately set up an ear-piercing wail.

It wasn't difficult to tell where the blast had taken place. Smoke rolled out of the kitchen under the door. A cloud of it billowed out as the door swung open, and from the cloud emerged little Ambrose, his hair sticking up and a big grin on his face beneath his Lone Ranger mask.

"Ambrose! What happened?" Danielle asked frantically as she rushed down the hall with Eudora bouncing in her arms, the baby's cry taking on a kind of yodeling quality as she ran.

"Tinks blowed up the macaroni surprise with a firecracker," he said with a giggle. "It was fun."

Bracing herself for the worst, Danielle pushed the kitchen door open and stepped in. Remy was standing near the table with a fire extinguisher in his hands. The table was lost somewhere under a sea of white foam. There was macaroni everywhere. It was stuck on the walls, on the white cupboards. Wiggling worms of macaroni dangled from the ceiling and the light fixture.

It was clear, though, that Tinks had got the worst of it. She stood at the head of the table looking like something from a cheap horror movie. Her face was covered with a slimy layer of cream of mushroom soup, dotted with bits of mushroom and crescents of overcooked pasta. Luckily, it appeared that the only thing seriously wounded was her pride. Her lower lip stuck out through the goo in a threatening pout.

Eudora, on the other hand, had stopped crying. She stared around the room, her blue eyes round with wonder as she took in the sight, as awestruck as if it were Christmas morning.

"Ah, me." Remy groaned, setting down the fire extinguisher. He speared both hands back through his dark hair as he picked his way across the macaroni-strewn floor toward the perpetrator of the crime. "What a mess!"

"Radical!" Jeremy exclaimed, bursting in through the door and bounding past Danielle. "Tinks slimed the kitchen!" He skidded across the slippery linoleum, pretending it was a skating rink.

Dahlia opened the door just enough to stick her head into the kitchen. Taking in the scene, she made a horrified face and squealed, "Gross! I'm gonna gag!"

With Eudora perched on her hip, Danielle tiptoed into the room, carefully tracing Remy's path to where he stood scraping Tinks off with a spatula.

"It would seem the caution inspired by the tales of your incarceration has worn off."

Remy said nothing, but scowled down at Tinks, his temper simmering.

From the hall on the other side of the kitchen Butler emerged panting, his hair disheveled, cheeks flushed. He looked to Remy as if he might have just run up the front stairs and down the back, but Remy made no comment other than a raised eyebrow at the Scot's shoes—a pair of black wingtips that looked very out of place beneath the legs of his pajamas.

"What the devil is going on here?" Butler demanded breathlessly. He tightened the belt of his robe and started forward into the room, remembering belatedly to stoop and press a hand to his back. "A man canna get a moment's peace in this house!"

"It was nothing, Butler," Danielle said reassuringly. "Just a minor explosion. You can go back to bed." She stopped herself and shook her head, a horrified look coming over her face. "What am I saying? *Just* an explosion? This isn't a household, it's a training facility for midget terrorists!"

Remy turned his attention back to Tinks, his big hands planted at the waist of his jeans, his shoulders looking impossibly huge as he leaned over her.

"You're in a whole lotta trouble, 'tite rouge. I want you upstairs an hour ago. Got it?"

Tinks gave him a mutinous glare. "You can't make me. I don't have to do what you say."

A muscle tightened and kicked in Remy's jaw. "You wanna take bets on that?"

She hauled back and kicked him in the shin a split second before he could grab her. Remy winced, biting his tongue on the string of expletives that threatened. Tinks turned to make a break for it, but Remy caught her around the waist and swung her up, spinning her around and plunking her over his shoulder like a sack of potatoes. Her breath left her on a surprised "Oof!" She tried to kick him once. He stilled her squirming with one hand shackling her ankles and one smacking her smartly on the fanny.

"We'll be upstairs discussing the new house rules regarding explosives," Remy said tightly to Danielle as he passed her, his face dark with fury, black eyes flashing.

Danielle, Eudora, and Jeremy watched them go. Jeremy looked stunned and pale, his freckles stood out in sharp relief against his skin. His eyes bugged out like Bart Simpson's. Butler looked thoughtful. Eudora gave a startled little gasp and pressed a chubby hand to her mouth as the kitchen door swung shut.

"Uh-oh is right, sweetheart," Danielle said, with a smile of smug admiration. "I think Tinks has met her match."

"Do you think he'll kill her?" Jeremy asked in a hushed tone. "Do you think he'll dunk her in chicken broth and feed her to the alligators?"

Danielle gave him a look. "Of course not. Mr. Doucet is a trained professional nanny."

Butler gave a snort at that, but declined to elaborate when Danielle turned toward him. She looked from his face to Jeremy's to Eudora's, her initial pleasure at Remy's actions fading. She might have wanted Tinks to have an attitude adjustment, but she certainly didn't want the little girl hurt, despite the many dire empty threats Danielle herself had made. She turned and stared at the kitchen door as if it were the portal to hell, her ears trained to catch the faintest sound of suffering. The house was ominously silent.

What did she really know about Remy Doucet? As paranoia tried to get a foothold in her mind, she walked calmly across the carpet of macaroni, not wanting everyone to panic.

"I think I'll take Eudora up to bed," she said, putting so much false serenity into her voice she sounded like she'd had a lobotomy. "Why don't you all go back to whatever you were doing?"

After depositing the baby in her crib, Danielle crept down the hall toward the sliver of light that escaped Tinks's room to fall across the darkened hall. The rumble of Remy's husky voice gradually came into focus as she sidled up against the wall beside the partially opened door and peeked in through the crack.

"You coulda been hurt. You coulda hurt one of your brothers or sisters. How would you have felt if Ambrose had got his head blown off?"

"I dunno," Tinks mumbled meekly. She sat perched on the edge of her bed, her head down, her hands folded in the lap of her yellow nightie. She had been efficiently washed down and her red hair combed back behind her ears. Remy stood before her with one leg cocked, his hands on his hips, a solemn, expectant look on his face. Tinks peeked up at him and dropped her head again. "Bad, I guess."

"You guess." Remy gave a snort. He raised neither his hand nor his voice, but he brought Tinks to the brink of tears with his next words, just the same. "He's your little brother and he loves you. You remember that the next time you go to do somethin' stupid."

"Yes, sir."

Danielle's eyes widened at her niece's respectful tone.

"And how do you think your *Tante* Danielle feels, you blowin' up the dinner she made for you?"

"But it was gross!"

Remy's expression quelled her protest. "I don't care if it tasted like dog food right outta the can. You hurt her feelings and you oughta be ashamed."

Danielle bit her lip, her own eyes filling with tears of sympathy for Tinks, pity for herself, and tenderness for Remy for him thinking about her feelings. He really was a sweet man. A sweet *young* man, but that didn't matter so much at the moment.

Tinks hung her head even farther and tried unsuccessfully to sniffle back her tears. Remy relented then and sat down beside her on the bed, gathering the little tomboy to him for a bear hug. Tinks wrapped her arms around his brawny neck and cried on his broad shoulder for a couple of minutes. Remy rocked her and murmured to her, his lips brushing her temple every so often. Finally he whispered something in her ear that made her giggle. She sat back on his lap and rubbed her eyes with her fists.

Remy tweaked her nose and winked at her. "Bedtime for you, *pichoutte*."

"What's that mean?" Tinks asked as she scrambled under the covers and Remy tucked her in.

"Little girl."

"Yuk!"

He chuckled and turned toward the door. Too late, Danielle jumped back from the opening. He had seen her clearly. Their eyes had met unerringly in that split second. She cursed her slowing reflexes. They were the first to go. Next she'd be asking people to talk into her good ear.

She turned to make a token attempt at escape, but

Remy caught her from behind when she was no more than three steps from Tinks's door.

"Spyin' on me boss?" he asked softly, his dark eyes twinkling as he neatly trapped her with her back to the wall. He planted a big hand on either side of her shoulders and leaned toward her, giving her a teasing, questioning look. "You checkin' up on me? Hmm?"

Danielle swallowed hard. The inside of her mouth seemed to have turned to cheesecloth the instant Remy had gotten too close. "I—um—well . . . you looked so angry . . ."

"I *was* angry," he admitted. "I've got a helluva temper, *chère*. But it's like that firecracker—one blast and it's all over."

"It's all over all right," Danielle said, seizing the opportunity to steer the conversation away from dangerous territory. "It's all over the kitchen. We'll be cleaning up macaroni until the Second Coming."

"I take it there's no housekeeper?"

"She ran off the day Suzannah and Courtland left. Said something about preferring to take a job as a tour guide in Beirut."

"Yeah, well, some people got no guts atall," he said dryly. "I'll take care of the kitchen tomorrow."

"Thanks." Danielle gave him a wry little smile of appreciation and apology. "Kids, cooking, cleaning. I guess you got more than you bargained for taking this job."

His expression softened as he gazed at her, his eyes looking like black velvet in the dim light of the hall. "I sure did, sugar," he whispered, stepping closer, gently pinning her to the wall with the weight of his solid, muscular body. "I sure did."

Danielle sighed at the feel of him settling against her. He caught the sigh with his mouth the instant before his lips touched hers. It was a gentle kiss, almost tentative at first. He rubbed his lips over hers, softly, giving her the chance to deny him. When she didn't, he took it a step further, tracing the line of her mouth with the tip of his tongue.

Danielle trembled at the effort to resist temptation, but she lost the battle. It had been too long. She had secretly yearned for this while trying to tell herself she didn't need it, could live without it. She had denied herself before, but she couldn't deny herself now. She couldn't deny Remy. Her mouth opened beneath his like a flower opening to the heat of the sun.

He groaned his satisfaction as he wrapped his arms around her and slid his tongue inside her mouth in a languid caress that sapped the strength from her knees. She sagged against him, an electric current of pleasure zipping along her nerves from the spot where his burgeoning arousal nudged her belly.

It felt so good to be wanted, to be touched. She'd lived the last year in a cocoon of solitude. Now her senses were awakening with a sharpness that nearly took her breath away. When Remy broke the kiss and put an inch of space between them, she nearly cried out.

Remy watched her face as Danielle's sanity returned by degrees. Her look of frustration gave way to surprise then to horror then to forced anger. She scowled at him, her dark eyebrows pulling together in annoyance, her wide mouth turning down at the corners.

"You followed me up here 'cause you were afraid I might actually hurt the little demolition expert, no?" he said, taking the offensive before she could tell him he shouldn't have kissed her. He damn well should have kissed her and he intended to go on kissing her. There was no point in arguing about it. "I think you like these kids more than you let on. I think you like 'em a lot."

He spoke the words like a challenge. Her scowl

darkened. She didn't want him to think she cared all that much about the little monsters her sister had saddled her with, but he could sense she did. He had seen it in her eyes as she'd held little Eudora. He'd seen it as he'd hauled Tinks out of the kitchen. It was there even now behind the ferocious glare she was directing at his keen insight.

"Bite your tongue," she said, pretending offense.

Remy waggled his eyebrows at her and backed toward the steps with a devilish grin. "I'd rather bite yours."

"I ought to fire you," Danielle threatened, trying her best to ignore the blast of heat that shot through her at his audacious suggestion. "You're insubordinate."

"Yeah, but I'm a helluva kisser, eh, *chère*?"

On that note of truth he turned and trotted down the grand staircase, whistling.

# Six

Danielle awoke with a start, jackknifing upright in bed and gasping for air. Her nightgown was soaked through with sweat. Shaking violently, she wrapped her arms around herself and held on. The room around her was cast in silvery light as a big New Orleans moon shone through the open drapes at the tall windows. Everything was still. Everything was quiet.

It took a moment for her to realize where she was and why she was there. The nightmare had seemed so real. She couldn't shake the feeling that she was in London, in the flat she'd rented in Kensington, facing the bitter accusations of a woman who had been her best friend. It was her punishment that that night should remain so vivid in her mind. Over a year had passed and still she could feel the chill of the night, the knife-edge of the words. She could still smell the scent of the darkroom chemicals that had hung in the air that night, and for an instant everything in the room took on the red haze of the safelight. She could feel the intensity that enveloped her when she worked, pulling around her like a blackout shade, cutting out all distractions that didn't pertain to her art. And the awful stillness that had later pierced through her like a lance plunged into her heart once more.

She jerked around toward the nightstand, automatically reaching for the monitor she had carried with her since arriving at the Beauvais house. It was gone.

Without trying to bring some measure of sanity into the muddle in her mind, Danielle threw back the covers and launched herself from the bed. She didn't stop to put on her robe or her slippers. The panic drove her directly out into the hall.

The house was quiet. It was past two o'clock in the morning. Everyone was asleep. Even the fiendish Jeremy was snug in his bed, dreaming his diabolical dreams. Danielle hurried down the hall, her heart pounding in her breast, her bare feet scuffing along the soft blue runner that covered the hallway. At the door to the nursery she paused and stood there shaking with dread for a fraction of a moment. Then she reached for the crystal knob with a violently trembling hand and let herself into the room.

On the same side of the house as her own room, the nursery was flooded with moonlight. The white furniture glowed with it. In the crib, Eudora lay on her tummy, her cheek pressed to the sheet, eyes closed peacefully, her little mouth a perfect O. Danielle dropped to her knees and stared at the baby, her fingers grasping the bars of the crib like a prisoner clutching at the cell door. She held her breath tight in her lungs as she stared at the baby. Her eyes burned as she held them open, watching for Eudora's back to rise and fall.

When she was certain the baby was breathing properly, she let out a ragged sigh, the worst of the tension draining from her with the expelled air.

The shakes returned full force then as she dragged the rocking chair into position beside the crib and crawled into it. They rattled through her like the aftershocks of an earthquake, each one taking a little more of her strength with it. She pulled her feet up onto the seat of the chair and wrapped her arms around her knees unconsciously trying to hold herself together.

Eudora was fine. Everything was all right. Nothing had happened in the time since Danielle had finally succumbed to the need for sleep. She had broken the vigil, but nothing had happened. This wasn't Kensington. This wasn't Ann Fielding's baby.

Gradually the trembling subsided and a blessed numbness drifted through her. Motionless, she sat and watched her niece sleep.

Remy watched from the doorway, his shoulder braced against the jamb. The light that fell upon her face illuminated a kind of pain he'd never known, had never seen. It was so stark, so bleak it took his breath away. She was curled in the chair in a posture designed to shut the world out, but her expression told him she hadn't been successful. He had the feeling that what was hurting her was coming from within and her defenses couldn't guard her against it.

"Danielle," he said softly.

Danielle pulled herself out of her private hell long enough to glance toward the door. She stared at Remy as if he were a trick of the moonlight. He leaned against the door frame with a masculine grace that was both casual and arrogant. His white oxford shirt hung open, revealing a pelt of dark hair swirling over the sculpted muscle of his chest. He was barefoot. His jeans were zipped but not buttoned. The waistband gaped in a little vee where the line of dark hair that bisected his belly disappeared from view. He was a prime example of the male of the species—

handsome, virile, strong, but tender. Too bad he was beyond her reach.

"Danielle," he said again when she turned away from him. He padded across the carpet to kneel down by her chair. "What are you doin' here?"

"Watching the baby," she whispered, never taking her eyes off Eudora.

"She's asleep."

"Hmmm."

"You oughta be too."

"I'm fine. What are you doing here?"

"It's my job. I thought I'd better take a peak to make sure she was resting. I never figured I should be checkin' on you too."

"I'm fine," she said again, but still she didn't look at him.

Remy sighed and combed a hand back through his disheveled hair. It would have been apparent to the densest of people that Danielle was not fine. She looked like she was hanging on by a thread. As exhausted as she had appeared to be, she should have been sleeping like a corpse, but here she sat, staring at Eudora Beauvais almost as if she were afraid to look away from the sleeping infant.

Her ash-blond hair was mussed around her head and shoulders in wild disarray. She made no move to smooth it. There were lines of strain around her mouth and one digging a crevice between her eyebrows. None of that did anything to diminish the fact that she was pretty. As she sat there looking cool and aloof in her lavender silk nightgown, Remy wanted to reach up and touch her. He wanted to pull her down onto the floor with him and make love to her on the plush carpet, but he throttled his desires. There was something wrong here and he was going to have to find out what it was before he could begin to help.

Rising to his feet, he held out a hand to Danielle.

She glanced at it, but turned her attention back to the baby.

"I'd rather just stay here, thank you. Feel free to go back to bed."

"'I'd rather just stay here, thank you,'" he said, parroting her prim tone. He didn't withdraw his proffered hand, but nodded toward the cushioned window seat. "Come sit with me, *chère*. Come tell ol' Remy what you're doin' here in the middle of the night when all good boss ladies should be sleepin'."

Danielle considered her predicament. Enough reason had returned that she knew he would think her very strange for insisting on remaining in the chair. Not enough had returned to allow her to leave the room. She had no intention of telling him why she had come in here, but it would only pique his curiosity if she refused to talk at all.

Finally she pushed herself out of the rocker. Taking an anxious look at Eudora, she moved toward the window seat and situated herself on the edge of the rose velvet cushion, her back straight, her gaze on the crib. Remy sat opposite her, his back against the wall, left foot planted on the cushion, right one on the floor. Danielle could feel him watching her, waiting for her to say something.

"I had a bad dream," she admitted, not looking at him because it was far from the whole truth.

"About Eudora?"

"I thought I would feel better if I came in here and sat with her."

Silence reigned for a few minutes. Danielle continued watching the baby. She wondered what Remy was thinking. She wondered if he would accept her explanation at face value or if he would try to dig deeper. And she struggled with the conflict within herself. A part of her wanted to tell him the truth. He seemed like such a caring person, an understanding person. But who would ever be able to understand what had happened that night in London? And who would ever be able to forgive her when she couldn't forgive herself? The risk of condemnation wasn't worth the momentary relief she would receive by unburdening herself.

Remy watched her quietly, thoughtfully. He pulled a cigarette out of his shirt pocket and planted it loosely between his lips, inhaling the faint fragrance of the unlit tobacco. The woman before him was a puzzle. She was wealthy, but with none of the airs he associated with breeding and money. She was independent, but he sensed a longing in her, a loneliness. She was confident, but insecure about what he considered to be the most mundane things—cooking and raising kids. She talked as if she would rather have taken a trip to the dentist than take care of her nieces and nephews, yet here she was keeping watch over Eudora in the dead of night like a guardian angel.

Rolling his cigarette between his fingertips, he said, "How come you don't have any babies of your own?"

Danielle started at the sound of his low, rough voice. Or perhaps it was his question that made her flinch. She ordinarily met that sexist query with a sharp "none of your business," but she supposed it was a valid question considering the circumstances.

"I guess I'm just one of those old-fashioned girls who believes in marriage first."

"And how come you've never married?"

Her smile was wistful. "The men who asked were never right and the right man never asked."

Remy pocketed his cigarette again and frowned. "Who is this right man?" he asked a bit gruffly, all his territorial instincts bristling like the ruff on a guard dog. "He got a name?"

"No," Danielle said, amusement distracting her from her watch. She turned a little and settled herself more comfortably on the bench. "I'm a Hamilton, remember? Mr. Right wouldn't be liable to last any longer than the time it would take to get all my monogrammed towels changed."

"You really believe in that curse business, don't you?"

"Oh, it's not the curse," she admitted. "I'm not an easy person to live with. I suppose I take after my father that way. I don't have a very good track record with men. I imagine it's because I'm an artist," she said, glancing back at the sleeping baby, her wry smile fading. "An artist is always married to her work first. It's an obsession. I haven't run across many men willing to play second fiddle to my muse."

Remy leaned forward slowly, a predatory light in his black eyes. His right hand came up to comb Danielle's hair back from her cheek. Anchoring his fingers in the silvery mass, he tilted her head back so she had to look up at him. "Mebbe you just haven't found one man enough to knock your muse for a loop," he drawled in a voice like liquid smoke.

His threat was implicit. He was man enough. Excitement sizzled through Danielle. It swirled around like a whirlpool low in her belly and burned in her breasts. A latent sense of recklessness awakened within her and urged her to lean into him, to press herself against the broad male chest that was covered with curling black hair. She could feel his body heat; it lured her closer, just as the sensuous curve of his lower lip lured her closer.

Crazy, she thought, fighting the primitive urgings of her body. Somewhere she managed to find a cocky smile as she said, "Men have tried and men have died."

"Oh, yeah?" Remy chuckled. His smile flashed in the dark like the blade of a pirate's knife. "Sounds like a challenge to me."

"Sorry, you don't meet the age requirement."

He made a face as he released her and sat back. "You're like a terrier with a rat on that age thing, aren't you? Must be a birthday loomin' on the horizon."

"The big four-oh, if you must know," she said, squaring her shoulders and lifting her chin. "There, I've said it. Now you can slink off and feel properly foolish for coming on to a woman old enough to be your—"

"Lover." The word was a caress coming from his mouth. He said it with all the heated passion the term implied. He said it with the kind of excitement that brought to mind images of rumpled sheets and sweat-slicked skin. Danielle's breath whistled out of her lungs. "So you got a coupla years on me, *chère*. What difference does it make? What's between us has got nothin' to do with age."

"You can say that now, but what will you say when you see my steel-belted foundation garments?" she quipped, swallowing hard as her head swam.

"Kinky." He grinned when she rolled her eyes at him. "You're really that bent outa shape about turnin' forty? What's the big deal? It's only a number. You're a long way from joinin' the prune juice set."

He was right about that. Any other year she would have said the same thing. Age had never mattered to her. It was just that forty was a more significant peak. She was going to be forty and what did she have to show for it? She had a successful career, but she hadn't pursued her career in search of success; she was an artist for the sake of art, not fame. She was wealthy, but she had been born that way; it was no achievement.

Maybe what was bothering her was the fact that in a matter of days she was technically going to be over the hill and she had nothing of significance to show for the climb. As she looked at Eudora she wondered if maybe she had begun to think that children were a way of gauging a life and she had none; she would never have any. She had her art, but her art would not lament her when she was gone.

"You're a beautiful woman, Danielle," Remy whispered.

"And you're the nanny," she countered, using a tone designed to put servants in their place. The trouble was, this Cajun rogue didn't know his place. His dark eyes flashed with a rebellious light as he continued to stare her down.

"What about you?" she asked. "Why aren't there a passel of little Doucets dogging your heels?"

Remy's expression grew thoughtful. He didn't have a very good answer for her question. The fact of the matter was he had always wanted a family, and he still planned on having one. Even though he enjoyed playing the carefree bachelor, he liked the idea of married life—the constancy, the stability, the comfort of a mate. And the truth was he could have had his pick from a number of lovely ladies. One in particular had made it more than clear that she would marry him in a minute if he would but ask the question. But he hadn't asked her and he wasn't sure why. Marie Broussard was exactly what he wanted in a wife—a pretty Cajun girl who shared his values. Problem was he had never quite been able to fall in love with Marie. He liked her fine, but he didn't love her, and he was too much the romantic to settle for less.

He sighed in reflection then raised his eyebrows and turned up the corners of his lips. "You wanna do somethin' to help that situation, *ma chère*?"

Instead of the witty rejoinder he expected, Danielle's eyes went bleak. She turned away from him. "I'm the last person you should ask."

This wasn't about the curse, he thought as he studied her. This wasn't about her upcoming birthday. They were back to the little matter of why she was sitting there in the dark tearing herself up when she should have been asleep.

"You've seen a small sample of my expertise with children," she said sardonically, the thickening in her voice ruining the effect of the sarcasm. "No one's ever going to nominate me for mother of the year."

She had to know herself better than he did, Remy thought; he'd only met her. But he found himself wanting to refute her statement. Maybe that was for his own benefit. Maybe he wanted Danielle to be more adept at motherhood than she really was. Or maybe he was simply responding to the sadness in her voice. Whatever the reason, he acted on his instincts and pulled her back on the window seat, paying no attention to her struggle to resist. He pulled her back into the vee of his legs and hugged her to his chest.

"Mr. Doucet!" she hissed, fighting in vain to pull away as his arms banded like steel around her midsection, beneath the fullest swell of her breasts. He held her as easily as he would have held little Ambrose.

"Hush," he commanded, giving her a squeeze to still her squirming. "You'll wake the baby."

"That should be the least of your worries."

"That threat's losin' its starch, sugar. You aren't gonna fire me; you need me too much. Now lean back here against ol' Remy and stop thinkin' those dark thoughts that haunt your pretty silver eyes."

His insight effectively took the wind from the sails of her indignation. She'd always believed she was a good enough actress to hide the pain, the self-doubt. He had seen through her shield with ease. And he was going to offer her comfort whether she liked it or not.

Slowly the stiffness melted out of her body and she sank back against him. He was as solid as a rock, as warm as a security blanket. It felt much too good to be in his arms. Nothing about this situation was proper, but nothing had ever felt so achingly right. She was too tired to fight it now. She let her head fall back against his chest, her face turning so that her cheek brushed against the soft mat of hair. She breathed deep of the warm, masculine scent of him, and sighed out the last of her resistance.

Remy pressed a kiss into the tangles of her hair and softly sang a few bars of what sounded to her like a Cajun lullaby. He had a wonderful voice. It was as smooth as good whiskey, as seductive as a kiss. Without even realizing it, she snuggled closer into his warmth and her eyelids slid to half-mast. Her gaze was still on the baby, but all the tension associated with that task had left her. She listened to Remy's voice, her brain idly attempting to sort through the words, but the Cajun dialect was as different from the French she had learned as Elizabethan was from modern English.

"What does that mean?" she asked softly, half waiting to hear words of love. Half hoping as her mind drifted into the shadows of sleep.

He smiled against her hair and whispered. "'Workin's too hard and stealin's not right.'"

A soft laugh left her on a puff of air as her eyes shut. "How unromantic."

"*Demander comme moi je t'aimais, ma jolie fille,*" he sang softly, changing tunes to suit her. *Ask me how much I love you, my pretty girl.*

His heart skipped curiously and he held his breath a minute, wondering if Danielle had noticed. But she had fallen sound asleep in his arms. She lay against him, as trusting as a child, as beautiful as an angel. She was all wrong for him—an *américaine* lady who roamed the world with a restless heart and a hunger for things he couldn't understand. She was the client his sister had warned him away from.

He tightened his arms around her and sighed into

her soft wild hair. She may have been all wrong for him, but she felt so right. According to the rules, he wasn't supposed to want her. *But then*, said the little devil on his shoulder, *you ain't never been much for rules*.

"*Mais non*, I haven't," he murmured, his grin lighting his face like a crescent moon.

# Seven

Danielle awoke slowly. During the course of her career she had gotten up at whatever hour was necessary for her to get the shot she wanted, but she was by nature a night person. When she had her choice the most strenuous morning activity she tackled was peeling her eyelids up far enough to focus on the alarm clock by noon. She hadn't voluntarily seen a sunrise since 1981.

An enormous weight fell across the bed, pinning her legs to the mattress. The antique mahogany four-poster rocked beneath her. Obviously, this was an earthquake and the ceiling had fallen on her, she thought, not moving an inch. She decided she could just as well sleep until a rescue team arrived to dig her out of the rubble.

The bed shook again. The weight on her legs crawled its way up toward her head. A long wet tongue slurped over her cheek.

"Wake up, Auntie Dan-L."

Danielle managed to raise one eyelid just enough to make out Ambrose standing beside the bed wearing

Smurf pajamas and a pair of black glasses with a big fake nose, bushy eyebrows and mustache attached. His ragged stuffed dog was tucked under his arm.

"Do you want Puppy Chow to kiss you again?"

She turned her head, coming face to face with the Old English sheepdog that had settled on the other pillow. He was as big as a pony and so shaggy the only feature of his head that stood out was the tip of his wet black nose. He slurped her again, point-blank.

"Ugh!" Pulling her pillow over her face as a shield, she spoke to her nephew through it. "Ambrose, this is not your dog."

"Uh-huh."

"No, it isn't." She forced her legs to drop over the side of the bed and struggled to sit up. "I distinctly remember your dog being brown."

The boy giggled as if she'd just said the silliest thing. He grabbed her limp hand and tugged. With wobbling legs and a fuzzy head, Danielle stood up and wandered around the elegant room like a zombie. She ran a hand over her tangled hair and tried to recall her return to bed the night before. The last thing she remembered was the sound of Remy's voice as he sang to her. Glancing back at the rumpled bed, she wondered if he had carried her to it from the nursery. Had he slipped her beneath the sheets, tucked her in, brushed a kiss to her lips?

Heat suffused her at the thought and she shuddered. She was too attracted to him. He was too tempting. He was too young.

She scowled at the reminder.

While she stood lost in thought, Ambrose went about in a businesslike manner, selecting clothes for her to wear, pulling garments out of the closet his mother used for storage. He trailed the clothes across the wild-plum carpet and handed them to Danielle. Automatically she put the articles on over her nightgown without paying any attention to what they were. Her brain had fallen back into the blissful blankness that hovered just above sleep. When she finished dressing, her nephew took her by the hand again and led her away from the bed where the sheepdog had begun chewing on her pillow. He piloted her through the door and down the hall, jabbering all the while about his plans for the day.

"Coffee," she mumbled like one transfixed. "Coffee."

Remy stood in the kitchen with Eudora tucked under one arm and a spatula in his other hand, tending a pan of scrambled eggs on the stove. He glanced up as the door swung open and Ambrose led Danielle in. The air turned hot in his lungs. He uttered a prayer for mercy as his every male molecule snapped to attention.

She looked like an expensive date from a house of ill repute. She wore the same short lavender nightgown she'd had on when he'd last seen her, but over it was a sheer black pegnoir trimmed in lace and belted at the waist with a wide leather strap. A flowered silk scarf was draped jauntily over one shoulder. Her shapely legs were bare to a breathtaking few inches above mid-thigh. One good deep breath and he'd know whether or not she slept in panties.

He could have peeked the night before when he'd carried her back to her room, but that wouldn't have been fair. He wasn't into ogling unconscious women.

Barely conscious now, she shuffled across the floor, her eyes mere slits in her face, chanting, "Coffee . . . coffee . . ."

Remy dropped his spatula and handed her the cup he'd poured for himself. She wrapped both hands around the ceramic mug and brought it to her lips as if it contained the elixir of life. The strong hot liquid seared a bitter path down her throat, leaving behind an aftertaste of chicory. It hit her stomach sizzling and boiling like a witch's brew. The caffeine went directly to her brain, jolting all the little gray cells to life. Her eyes snapped open looking twice their normal size. She stared down into the cup at coffee that was blacker than a bayou at midnight.

Her words came out on a thin breath. "It's a little s-s-strong."

"Good, yes?" Remy said. He leaned close, bracing a hand on the counter on either side of her. He had put Eudora down on the freshly scrubbed floor. The baby crawled off happily in search of toys. "Like coffee oughta be. You like it?"

Danielle managed a wan smile. "Let's say you're not exactly Mrs. Olson."

"Yeah," he drawled, as he shifted his hips and shuffled a little nearer. "Ain't you glad?"

A giddy twitter was her only answer.

"That's a helluva an outfit you got on, *chère*," he said in his dark velvet voice. His black eyes glittered as his smile cut across his face. "You tryin' to tell me somethin'?"

Danielle glanced down at herself. Her jaw dropped so hard it nearly bruised her chest. She looked like she was ready to interview for a job on Bourbon Street. "Holy smoke!"

"My sentiments exactly," he agreed in a lazy drawl. His mustache tugged upward on the right as he let his gaze slide down over her again.

"Doesn't Auntie Dan-L look pretty?" Ambrose asked proudly. "I picked her clothes out myself."

Remy grinned. "You're a man after my own heart, Ambrose. That's a fabulous outfit."

Ambrose beamed behind his goofy glasses. "You really think so?"

"Oh, yeah . . ." His voice dropped another heart-stopping step. "Absolutely."

Danielle turned burgundy in spite of the fact that she thought she was too old to blush. She carefully removed Remy's arm from her path, her stomach flipping over at the feel of muscle and crisp dark hair under her fingertips. She kept an eye on him as she moved prudently away.

He was dressed again in jeans that accented every masculine inch of his lower body, displaying to blatant perfection the impressive part of his anatomy that made him male. Spanning his mile-wide shoulders was a khaki T-shirt emblazoned with a smirking alligator hawking beer. No one had a right to look so sexy so early in the day, Danielle thought crossly as she headed for the door.

"Oh, Danielle," he called. "Would you please pick up that toy car there on the floor before someone trips on it?"

She started to bend over automatically, but caught herself at the feel of her nightgown climbing up the backs of her thighs. She straightened and leveled a narrow-eyed look over her shoulder. "Not a chance, Doucet."

He shrugged and grinned an irrepressibly boyish grin. "Can't blame a guy for tryin'."

No, she couldn't blame him for trying. She blamed herself for wanting him to try. How was she going to get through the next two and a half weeks, she wondered as she showered.

She needed a distraction even more powerful than Remy's male allure. She pondered over that seemingly impossible quest as she dressed in knee-length navy-blue shorts and a prim white sleeveless cotton blouse with a Peter Pan collar. She picked up the scarf Ambrose had chosen for her and fingered the whisper-soft silk. It wasn't that she was falling for the kid, she told herself as she used the scarf to secure her hair at the nape of her neck. Sure, she wasn't falling for Ambrose any more than she was falling for Remy Doucet.

Brother, was Suzannah ever going to pay for this!

But revenge would come later. Now she needed a distraction. She needed . . . work. Work! That was it. Few things had ever been able to cut through the concentration she poured into her work. All she had to do was hang a camera around her neck and it would act as a talisman to ward off virile younger men who had no business coming on to her. Virile younger men who sang to her and held her and kissed like bandits, stealing every scrap of common sense she possessed. Virile younger men with dark Cajun voices and pirates' smiles.

Her knees wobbled and her resolve swayed ominously as she rushed to the darkroom where Courtland Beauvais developed his own black and white prints as a hobby. She unlocked the door with the small key that was always left on top of the door frame and fell to her knees on the cool linoleum floor beside her own battered camera bags.

Work. Blessed, glorious work. She would do a perspective of New Orleans. The architecture of New Orleans. No, she needed something more focused than that. The doorways of New Orleans. Yes, that was it. Doorways. She'd do them by sections—the French Quarter, the Garden District, Bourbon Street and Magazine Street. She sighed with relief as a flood of images washed through her brain. This was the perfect diversion. Work was her life, after all.

Ignoring the pang of emptiness that thought brought on, she slipped the camera bag over her shoulder and headed for the stairs.

Remy sat at the kitchen table lingering over another cup of killer coffee and the business section of the *Times-Picayune*. There wasn't a Beauvais in sight. The only sound was the bouncy zydeco music coming from the radio on the counter. Danielle thought the raucous accordion music very nearly drowned out the pounding of her pulse when Remy glanced up and assessed her new outfit with a slight frown.

"Where are the kids?"

"Gone swimmin'. All except the baby. She's down for a nap."

Great. Danielle groaned inwardly. The children were gone, out of the house, out of the picture. She was essentially all alone with Remy Doucet, Cajun hunk of the year. Terrific, she thought with a sinking feeling as she lowered her camera bag to the floor. Where were those rotten kids when she needed them? Her gaze ran around the room in the attempt to find something to look at besides Remy.

"How did you get this room so clean so fast?" She hadn't noticed on her initial trip into the kitchen, but there wasn't a trace of last night's disaster. She couldn't spot a single worm of macaroni anywhere. No one coming into the room now would have guessed her dinner had been so inedible the children had felt compelled to blow it up.

"I told the kids they had to help me or they couldn't go swimmin' with their friends."

"Extortion." Danielle nodded her approval. "Why didn't I think of that?"

She poured herself half a cup of coffee and filled the mug the rest of the way with tap water. One sip of Cajun coffee had been enough. With a belated look of disbelief she slid down onto a chair kitty-corner from Remy at the table. "The Beauvais kids have friends?"

"Saw them with my own eyes. Hard to believe, isn't it?"

"Oh," she said on a wistful sigh. "I guess they have their moments when they seem almost humanoid."

Remy studied her expression as she gazed off into space. He set his paper aside and leaned his forearms on the table. "They're not so different from regular kids. They just need a little discipline is all."

"You're very good with them," Danielle said, trying

to sound like a boss complimenting an employee. Recalling lessons in deportment, she sat straight in her chair as she sipped her watered-down coffee and nibbled on a beignet. "How did you become interested in being a nanny?"

Remy glanced away guiltily. She wasn't likely to be pleased if he told her he'd taken the job on a dare. He didn't like lying to her either. He swallowed hard as the noose he'd made tightened around his throat. The little devil on his shoulder came to the rescue.

*You don't have to lie. Just don't tell the truth.*

"Oh, well," he began, his roguish grin firmly in place once again. "There's lots of Doucets back on the Bayou Noir. I've been takin' care of nieces and nephews and cousins and all for years. It's sort of a family calling, don'tcha know. My sister Giselle has made a great success of her agency here in N'Awlins." And she will whip my sorry behind if I screw this up, he reminded himself. "I'm countin' this all as good practice for when I have kids of my own, aren't you?"

"Me?" Danielle fidgeted on her chair. "What would I do with kids?"

"Love them," he said simply.

Dodging his steady dark gaze, she tore off a crumb of beignet and ate it, daintily licking powdered sugar from the tip of her index finger. Love them. Didn't he know that love wasn't always enough? Obviously not. He was talented with children. The talented could never quite understand how special their gift was or how rare. Perilously close to falling into melancholy, Danielle fought off the feeling with dry humor. "How could I have kids? I'd need a bigger apartment, more luggage, a man."

"You asking for volunteers?" Remy's eyes lit up. His voice dropped a sexy notch. "Go put that other outfit back on and we'll talk."

"Somehow I don't think that costume would inspire much talk," Danielle said dryly.

"No," he agreed with a predatory smile. "But it sure would inspire a whole lotta action."

Making a supreme effort to bring the conversation back to a nonsexual level, Danielle put on her best business face and said, "I'm normally on the road. My work isn't conducive to home and hearth."

Remy frowned. "It sounds to me like your life isn't conducive to anything but loneliness."

The accuracy of his observation stunned her. And it surprised her. She had never considered her life lonely. She had friends and colleagues all over the world. She loved her work. But what she had lived with over this past year was exactly what Remy had said—loneliness, loneliness that had little to do with the solitary life she'd led in Tibet; it went much deeper than that. His statement also unnerved her, but she wasn't about to let him see that.

"I love my life," she said. "I get restless stuck in one place too long. I love to travel, see the world, meet people."

"So I guess you'll be leavin' N'Awlins once Mrs. Beauvais gets back."

She pushed her chair back from the table and stood. "There's nothing holding me here."

Before she realized what was happening, Remy was out of his chair and she was wrapped in his arms, up to her ears in Cajun charm. His pirate's grin slashed across his dark face and his ink-black hair tumbled across his forehead as he bent her back over his hard-muscled arm. "I'm holding you here, darlin'. Wanna dance?"

"You're a lunatic," Danielle said breathlessly, amazed at his mercurial change of mood. She thought she was going to melt where her thighs pressed to his. He was as solid as an oak tree and as easily moved. Her struggling only resulted in bringing her into even more intimate contact with him, her pelvis arching into his as she pressed her palms against his chest for leverage. She scowled at him. "If I hadn't been so desperate, I would have checked your references."

He quirked a brow. "Desperate for me? I like the sound of that."

"Oh, yeah? Do you like the sound of bones breaking? I'm going to punch you if you don't let me go."

He straightened, flung her out away from him by one arm, twirled her around and pulled her back into his arms so that she landed with a thud against his chest—if anything, even closer than she had been before. He adopted a look much too innocent to be trusted. "You'd punch me out for giving you a dance lesson?"

"Dance lesson, my foot."

Her heart had gone on a rampage, pounding against not only her breast but Remy's as well. She could feel the sharp rise and fall of his chest as he, too, struggled for a good deep breath. Knowledge that he was every bit as aroused as she was only served to heighten the excitement she was trying to fight. She had sworn to herself she was going to stay away from him, but she hadn't been pressed up against his body at the time. If that wasn't enough to make a woman willing to throw caution to the winds, nothing was.

The music coming from the radio had turned sultry. "Yellow Moon," a sexy song by the Neville Brothers, a song that inspired swaying hips, a song designed to ignite forbidden fires—as if her fires needed any additional fuel, Danielle thought. Remy's body picked up the rhythm of the music and he began to move automatically, almost absently, as if dancing were as natural to him as walking.

"Let's go dancin' tonight. Beausoleil's at the Maple Leaf."

"What about the kids?" Danielle asked breathlessly, caught up in the seductive sway of his body and the feel of his big hands on the small of her back.

"We'll get a sitter."

She planted her feet firmly on the linoleum and gave him a look. "*You're* the sitter."

Remy made a face and dipped her. "Such a stickler for details, angel. Loosen up. This is N'Awlins, darlin', the Big Easy. *Laissez les bons temps rouler*—let the good times roll. You gotta go dancin' while you're in N'Awlins. I think it's a city ordinance."

"I'm in trouble then, aren't I?" she said, refusing the call of his senuous movements and resolutely keeping her sneakers rooted to the floor.

"Don't worry. I'll teach you."

"Do you value your feet?"

"Only when I need 'em to walk." His jet eyes gleamed with mischief and his dimple cut deep into his cheek. "If you cripple me too bad, I guess I'll have to spend all my time in bed."

"Think how lonely you'll be," she said, gritting her teeth as her knees began to sway of their own volition.

With his eyes locked on hers, Remy lowered his head and nipped at her lower lip. His voice was as dark and textured as rumpled black satin sheets. "Not if you're there with me, *chère*."

Chemistry is an amazing thing, Danielle reflected dimly as Remy's mouth settled on hers. All Remy had to do was touch her and steam rose. The hot haze of passion clouded her mind, obscuring all thoughts of age and propriety and safety. She forgot she didn't have much luck with men, that she had, for all intents and purposes, given them up. The heat Remy generated against her and within her burned everything else out of her mind.

She melted against him, sighing as he deepened the kiss with masterful strokes of his tongue. Her head swam with the taste and scent of him—warm, dark, utterly masculine, coffee-flavored. Shivers showered down her body as his mustache tickled her upper lip. He laid claim to her mouth with a predatory possessiveness, probing, stroking. His right hand slid from the small of her back up and around her rib cage to claim her swelling breast. He cupped her, kneaded her, groaned into her mouth as his thumb flicked across her nipple. Pressing gently against the tightly knotted flesh, he rubbed in circles, sending shock waves through Danielle that reached clear to her toes.

She found her own hands wandering over the broad expanse of his back, exploring the planes and ridges of hard muscle through the fabric of his T-shirt. It was both exciting and frustrating. She wanted to feel his flesh, bare and warm. She wanted nothing separating her from experiencing the flex and strain of his muscles beneath his smooth skin. His shirt was denying her the privilege and that denial only served to sharpen what was already a rampant hunger.

She discovered the hem and reached beneath it as Remy backed her into the kitchen table. Her hips bumped against the edge of it and she automatically raised up on tiptoe to half sit on the polished pine. Remy nudged her knees apart, stepping in between her legs and pressing himself intimately against her. Danielle raked her short fingernails against his back as he rubbed his erection against her in the same rhythm as he thrust his tongue into her mouth.

The message was unmistakable and irresistible. Still he dragged his mouth to her ear and murmured, "Oh, Danielle, I want you. Let me love you, *chère*. Let me please us both."

Danielle groaned at the raw desire in his voice. It echoed her own. She wanted him more desperately than a five-year-old wants Christmas. Her blood was searing her veins and the heat was pooling into liquid warmth between her thighs. His hips moved against hers insistently. His strong, blunt-tipped fingers massaged her breast. She had no idea how things had gotten so out of control so quickly, but then she was beyond reason.

Remy's hand slid down from her breast to the waistband of her shorts and he deftly popped the button from its mooring.

"No," she whispered, her fingers closing over his before he could lower her zipper. For an instant she almost thought she was going to try to stop him, then her mouth said, "Not here."

Remy turned her hand and brought it against the front of his jeans, cupping her fingers around his sex and groaning as she stroked him through the denim. "We'll go to my room," he growled through his teeth. "It's closer."

"Good day all!" a falsely cheerful voice boomed from the doorway to the back hall.

"Butler!" The name burst from Danielle's lips like a curse. She leaped away from the table and folded her hands nervously at her waist. "What are you doing out of bed?"

"Stoppin' us from gettin' into it," Remy muttered under his breath. He snatched up the folded newspaper he had left on the table and held it in front of him, trying to look casual. He sent the Scot a fierce scowl.

"I thought it might do me good to move around a wee bit," Butler said. He tightened the sash on his tartan robe and moved gingerly into the kitchen.

"Yeah," Remy agreed, a muscle tightening in his square jaw. "Mebbe you oughta take a *long* walk. Call us when you get to Baton Rouge, we'll come pick you up."

Butler made no comment, but sent him a cool look brimming with smug triumph.

"The children have gone swimming," Danielle said, moving to the counter to pour the butler a cup of Remy's paint-stripping coffee—and to fasten her shorts unobtrusively. "You should have taken advantage of the peace and quiet and rested."

He accepted the mug and raised a pious eyebrow at Remy. "The young charges off swimming and the nanny didna go with them?"

"The nanny stayed here with the baby," Remy said stiffly.

"Indeed," Butler said doubtfully. "With the mistress as well." His gaze dropped to the younger man's hands. "Is that today's paper?"

"Yesterday's," Remy said through his teeth. "Not good for anything but wrappin' fish."

Danielle blushed at the thought of the whopper that paper was presently protecting. Trophy-size. Suitable for mounting. The heat of embarrassment spread out to the tips of her ears. How could she have let Remy get her into such a compromising position? She knew better. Lord, she'd nearly made a fool of herself right smack on her sister's kitchen table! She had to be losing her mind. Senility, that's what it was, the onset of Alzheimer's. She couldn't get involved with a man like Remy Doucet, a man with roots and a yearning for a family.

Her eyes fastened on the camera bag she had abandoned earlier and she fell on it like a drowning woman on a life preserver. Hefting the bag up, she settled the strap on her shoulder and started toward the door. The two men snapped out of their scowling match, their head swiveling in unison toward her.

"Lass?"

"Hey, where you goin', sugar?"

"To work," she said, steeling herself against the looks of disappointment that were being leveled at her for different reasons. "Where I belong."

# *Eight*

Danielle managed to escape Remy and the kids all day. After leaving the house in the morning she wandered the City That Care Forgot, doing her darnedest to forget her own cares. It was a fruitless effort. Even though she had cursed Suzannah's grand plan that she be a "family influence," even though she had hired a nanny with every intention of abandoning said nanny with the children, she felt guilty. It was insane, but she sort of missed the sound of death threats and crying.

She walked the few blocks to Magazine Street where she spent the better part of the day photographing the doorways of antique shops. When images of Remy clouded her view, she quickly reminded herself that she was not far from being eligible to join the pricey old merchandise that filled the display windows.

Many of the brick buildings along the street dated back to the seventeen and eighteen hundreds. Their doorways were works of art. They weren't simply the entrances to businesses, they were the faces of buildings that had seen Spanish rule and French, pirates and belles, soldiers and carpetbaggers. They were archways to other eras.

It was a working day, and the shops were open, but the intensity of the heat and humidity had kept most sane people indoors. That suited Danielle fine; she wasn't feeling a bit sane. She blocked the sultry weather from her mind. So it was ninety-five in the shade and she could have cut the air with a machete. Sweat ran in rivulets between her breasts and down her back. It was nothing compared to the steamy scene she'd shared with Remy in the kitchen. She pulled a battered khaki cap from her camera bag and tugged it on. The subtropical sun couldn't fry her brain any worse than Remy's kisses had.

She was disgusted to find that the concentration she had always been famous for seemed to be eluding her. More often than not she found herself distracted from a shot by thoughts of Remy; mostly choice memories of their near miss on the kitchen table.

It wasn't like her to lose her head that way, she mused as she picked at a scrumptious-looking seafood po'boy sandwich late in the afternoon. She sat at a little wrought-iron table in a sidewalk café in the French Quarter. The bottle of cold mineral water she had ordered went down easily, but she nibbled at the edges of the sandwich like a mouse, not really tasting the freshness of either the bread or the tiny shrimp.

The restlessness within her was a terrible thing. It wasn't the same thing she felt when some faraway place beckoned her muse. This was altogether different. It was almost the same inner turmoil that had driven her from London. She hated this tormenting demon, yet felt almost powerless to resist its command.

Damn Suzannah, she thought, tearing off a bit of bun and tossing it to a pigeon that had come to beg at her feet. If it hadn't been for her half-sister, she would have been off in a place where no one could bother her . . . or depend on her, or expect anything more of her than clicking the hours away with a camera in her hands.

The routine Danielle fell into over the next two days was exhausting, but it effectively kept her away from the Beauvais house. Or, more precisely, away from the inhabitants of the Beauvais house. She rose at the crack of dawn, escaping with camera equipment in tow and returned at the children's bedtime, when Remy was preoccupied. She would bid everyone a good night and then sequester herself in the darkroom past midnight. In the small hours of the morning, she would slip into Eudora's room and watch the baby sleep. She would get precious little sleep herself, dozing off and on, until it was time to start the whole routine over.

The grueling routine kept her away from Butler's too-watchful eye. It kept her away from the children. It kept her away from the temptation of Remy. It was also making her miserable and exhausted. Her nerves were shot. She felt guilty. She felt as if something in her chest were tearing in two. The only way she kept going was by reminding herself it would all be over in two weeks and promising herself she would then crawl off somewhere and sleep for a solid month.

"Or maybe two," she muttered to herself as she hauled her gear up the curving grand staircase and headed down toward the darkroom on the third night of her ordeal.

"Auntie Dan-L!" Ambrose called, scrambling out of his bedroom as she passed. He ran up to her wearing his Smurf pajamas and a Mardi Gras mask made out of blue feathers. His stuffed dog was tucked under his arm. A real dog—a brown and white terrier—scampered along at his feet. The pair skidded to a halt before her. "Where have you been all day?"

"Working. Ambrose, that isn't your dog. What happened to the big shaggy one?"

Ambrose ignored her question in the way only children can. "You work all the time. You missed the fun. Mr. Butler went out to sit in the garden and Tinks bombed him with a water balloon. Splat!" His face lit up with glee as he used his hands to demonstrate the explosion. "Mr. Remy laughed, but I'm the only one that saw him; it's my secret. And then Jeremy put a sock down the toilet and it flooded all over. Dahlia gagged."

Danielle was too weary to fight her smile. She knelt down and ruffled the boy's bright hair. "Sounds like you had quite a day."

"Yup. I missed you, though. I wish you'd stay more."

A lump the size of a Bermuda onion lodged in Danielle's throat at her nephew's candid admission. Ambrose missed her. Sentiment gushed over the dam of her resolve and swamped her. "I missed you too," she whispered.

"Then why do you have to work? Why can't you be with us?"

"It's kind of complicated, Ambrose," she said. It had to do with wanting things she couldn't have and doing something for the greater good of all concerned. She only wished it didn't have to hurt so much.

There was suddenly a thunder of footsteps on the stairs. Danielle turned to see Tinks and Jeremy barreling toward her, looking as if they had just escaped some unnamed terror by the skin of their teeth.

"Hi," Jeremy said between gasps for breath. His eyes fastened on the door behind Danielle, then turned to her. "Can me and Tinks come in the darkroom with you?"

Danielle shook her head, though she was secretly pleased they wanted to spend time with her. Maybe she wasn't as big a flop with kids as she thought. Ambrose missed her. Jeremy and Tinks wanted to be with her. "Nope. Sorry. You know the rules about the darkroom—absolutely no kids allowed. There's too much stuff in there that could hurt you."

Jeremy gave her his best pleading look as Tinks stole a nervous glance over her shoulder. "Aw, come on, Auntie Danielle. Please. It'd be so cool."

Danielle felt herself relenting, but she didn't give in. As much as she wanted the kids to like her, she had to think of safety first. A darkroom full of chemicals was no place for an insatiably inquisitive nine-year-old and his anything-on-a-dare little sister. "Nope. I can't let you, guys."

They were about to really start begging when heavier footsteps sounded on the stairs. Tinks and Jeremy both went a little pale beneath their freckles. The terrier whined. Ambrose giggled.

Remy appeared on the landing like an avenging Cajun god—big, dark, and brooding. His gaze flicked over Danielle but homed in quickly on Tinks and Jeremy. As he stalked down the hall, his expression ominous, he raised a hand and pointed at the pair.

"You two, back to the kitchen. Don't you be makin' me any more ticked off than I already am or I'll hand you over to my brother Lucky and let him use you for gator bait."

Without a word, Jeremy and Tinks scooted past him and disappeared down the stairs. Danielle swallowed the disappointment she felt at discovering the children had only wanted to use her and the darkroom for a hideout.

"What have they done now?" she asked, pushing herself to her feet.

Remy planted his hands on his hips and gave her a wry look. "You know that oil portrait of the Beauvais who fought beside Andrew Jackson in the Battle of N'Awlins?"

"The one that hangs in Courtland's study?"

"*Oui*, the very one. The Dynamic Duo decided he'd look better with a mustache and a goatee."

Danielle's face dropped. "They didn't."

"They did. In indelible laundry marker. They are now supposed to be pondering the error of their ways as they scrub the kitchen floor with toothbrushes."

"Mr. Butler got *really-eally* mad," Ambrose added, his eyes bugging out behind his mask.

Remy grimaced at the reminder of Butler, the bane of his existence. Checking his watch, he said, "It's past your bedtime, *'tit chaoui*."

"That means little raccoon," Ambrose explained to Danielle with no small amount of pride. He tugged on her hand so she would bend down for a good-night kiss, then trotted back to his room with the day's mystery dog right behind him.

The instant the boy disappeared Danielle became painfully aware of the fact that she was alone with Remy for the first time since their infamous shake-and-bake kitchen scene. She pulled her camera bag into her arms and hugged it to her.

"Well," she said, her mouth cotton-dry, gaze aimed just to the left of Remy's head. "Guess I'd better get to work. I'm glad to know you're handling everything here while I'm out."

"Oh, I'm real good at handlin' things," he said, his dark voice dripping insinuation. He smiled a little to himself as he watched the color bloom across her gorgeous cheekbones. "Can *I* come in the darkroom with you, Danielle? I'm a big boy."

Was he ever, she thought, not quite able to keep her gaze from flicking hungrily over his muscular frame. Heat swept through her, making a mockery of the mansion's central air-conditioning. "I don't think so," she stammered. "I don't like distractions when I'm working."

Attempting to dismiss him, she turned and took the key down from its hiding place and unlocked the door. He wasn't leaving; she could feel him standing right behind her. "Good night," she mumbled, slipping into the darkroom. She tried to pull the door shut behind her, but one big sneakered foot prevented her.

"This once," Remy said with a boyish grin. "I wanna see what you been doin' all day besides avoiding me."

He muscled his way into the narrow room that had at one time been a gentlemen's dressing room. Danielle scowled at him. "Have you ever considered a career in selling door-to-door?"

Ignoring her sardonic question, he set about exploring the darkroom, keeping one eye on Danielle. She didn't like him trespassing on her private territory and stood in the far corner bristling like a cat. Well, that was just too bad, he thought as he poked around, examining the tanks, print trays, the various bottles of mysterious solutions, the enlarger, the print dryer—the tools of the trade she claimed to prize above all else. He had his doubts about that, but he was going to keep them to himself for the moment.

He'd found several books of her work prominently displayed in the Beauvais library and had studied them intently over the past few days. Even his untrained eye could recognize Danielle's brilliance. She had a wonderful talent for capturing the essence of each person she photographed. The life and thoughts of her subjects were there for all to see—joy, sorrow, innocence, pride, even the most complex mix of emotions came through with striking clarity. Her photographs were so vivid, so true-to-life, they seemed almost three-dimensional.

Her book *Americans* had more than once nearly moved him to tears. A World War II veteran holding hands with the son who had lost his legs in Vietnam as a Memorial Day parade passed before them. A Midwestern farmer and his wife dancing joyously in their yard, arms raised to the heavens as rain poured down to end a summer drought. A homeless woman on the streets of San Francisco holding her child on her lap, her pride shattering as she begged a stranger for spare change.

These were not the photographs of a woman who valued art above all else. These had come from the genius of a woman who was perhaps a bit too sensitive, too insightful. She had laid her own soul bare in her work, and Remy had found himself falling a little more in love with her. He even found himself able to forgive her for abandoning him to the wiles of a dour Scot and a gang of kids destined for reform school.

"If you're through snooping," Danielle said sharply. "I have work to do."

"Mmmmm . . ." he hummed, working his way back to her corner.

If the lady thought he was going to allow her to avoid him indefinitely after their incomplete chemistry experiment in the kitchen, then she would have to think again. He'd never experienced that kind of spontaneous combustion in his life, and he was willing to bet Danielle hadn't either. That was part of the reason she'd run off, he was sure. It had frightened her to lose control that way. It had excited the hell out of him, but then he wasn't terrified about getting involved. He had decided to let her dodge him for a couple of days, hoping she would come around to his way of thinking. But it looked as if she'd go on running forever if he didn't put a stop to it.

"Are these the pictures you've been taking?" he asked, pulling a stack of black and white photographs off a shelf.

"Feel free to look them over," she said, crossing her arms over her chest.

There had to be a hundred, eight-by-tens and five-by-sevens, light, dark, taken from every conceivable angle. Every one of them of a doorway and nothing more. Photo after photo of closed doors. Remy sorted through them, frowning, his brows drawing together and etching a little worry line into his forehead as he pondered their meaning.

"There's no people in these," he said slowly.

"Darn—knew I forgot something," she said. She slapped her forehead with the palm of her hand. "How absentminded of me." Scooting around him, careful not to touch, she set about preparing everything for developing yet another five rolls of uninspired doorway photos.

Remy set the stack of pictures back where he'd found them and studied Danielle intently as she poured developer into the tank and checked the thermometer to make sure the temperature was within range. "Why no people?"

"Because I didn't feel like taking pictures of people."

"But you always take pictures of people—people in Tibet, Bora Bora, Des Moines. . . ."

She passed the comment off with a shrug, trying not to take any delight in the fact that he'd been studying up on her.

"You ought to have had people in them."

"Everybody's a critic," she mumbled, too aware that in one corner of her mind she knew he was right. More than once a part of her had prodded her to snap the doorway when a happy patron was leaving a shop with a treasure, or when a bored salesgirl had come out for a breath of air, or when the owner's wife had set out a bowl of milk for some sleek stray cat. But she hadn't taken those pictures. She had waited until the door had closed.

She nervously glanced around. The equipment and chemicals were ready, but she couldn't proceed without turning off the ordinary light and flipping on the dim red safelight, which didn't seem like a good idea at all with Remy in the room.

"I'm takin' the kids to the zoo tomorrow," he said. "Seems to me you got enough pictures of empty doorways to last a while. Come along with us."

She gave him a look. "Spend a day at the zoo with the Beauvais kids? What fun. Couldn't I just stay home and hit my thumb with a hammer?"

"What are you afraid of, sugar? That you might actually enjoy it?" he asked, the light of challenge in his eyes.

That was *exactly* what she was afraid of, but there was no way she would admit it to Remy. She would only be in deeper if she confided in him. There was too much room for error, for rejection, for pain. Taking her cue from him, she simply didn't answer, but went to dig her cameras out of her bag. "How was Butler today? Is his back getting any better?"

Remy rolled his eyes and snorted. "That man is a royal pain in the posterior."

"He happens to be very good at what he does."

"Layin' around and complainin'? *Mais* yeah, I don't guess I've ever seen anybody better at it. He's a master, he is."

"Oh, you're just sore because he interrupted us—" She cursed herself for resurrecting the subject and the memory. Heat flashed through her in a quick burst.

"Sore is a good word," Remy said lazily. He trapped her against the counter with an arm on either side of her and very deliberately snuggled his pelvis up against her bottom, drawing an involuntary gasp from Danielle. "I've still got that ache, *chère*," he said on a low groan. "And now that we're alone mebbe you'll help me do somethin' about it."

"I don't think so." Her voice came out much thinner than she had intended, much less resolute.

"Why not?" Remy asked, deftly turning her in his arms so she could no longer hide her face from him. "I'm attracted. You're attracted. We're both mature adults."

"Some of us more mature than others," she muttered.

Annoyed, Remy snagged a hand in her ponytail and tilted her head back so she had to look him in the eye. "Don't give me that age crap, Danielle. If it doesn't matter to me, then it shouldn't matter to you."

"Well, it does matter to me. I don't think we should get involved."

"That's the trouble with you, angel," he said on a growl. "You think too damn much."

His kiss was hot and hungry. He slanted his mouth across Danielle's with a sense of purpose that sent shock waves to her most feminine parts. To her shame, she did nothing to stop him. Her traitorous needs pushed aside the fears and the doubts and the sense of self-preservation, as she greedily took what Remy offered. As if a switch had been flipped, she stopped thinking and let herself feel.

It was a powerful and frightening force, this desire that sprang up inside her. It was like nothing she'd ever known, and that scared her. If she had never felt this way before in nearly forty years, she thought, chances were she would never feel this way again. This one man might be the only man, and he was all wrong for the kind of life she had chosen.

But none of that mattered now when Remy's mouth was on hers, when his tongue urgently sought out hers. Sinking into bliss, Danielle let herself revel in the experience of kissing him. She soaked up every sensation as if it had been years since he'd last touched her. She enjoyed the brush and tickle of his mustache, the coffee-flavored taste of him, the power in his brawny arms as he held her. She curved her body into his to better feel the hard masculine contours of him, to arch against the evidence of the passion she inspired in him.

Without breaking the kiss, she reached an arm behind her and fumbled blindly with the panel of light switches. Soft white gave way to the hazy red of the safelight, and Danielle thought dimly that she would never feel quite the same way about working under that light again. That soft glow of red would ever after bring to mind hot Louisiana nights and the taste of black coffee and the feel of strong arms.

*"Ah, chère, j'aime te faire l'amour avec toi,"* Remy murmured, trailing kisses down the column of her throat as his hands swept up her sides to claim her breasts through the soft peach-colored T-shirt she wore.

She didn't have to understand the words to understand their meaning. He wanted her. She wanted him. With common sense suddenly nowhere in sight, Danielle wasn't sure she could come up with a reason to stop from giving in this time.

As it turned out, she didn't have to. Someone on the other side of the darkroom door did it for her. At the sound of the knock Remy turned and kicked the baseboard, swearing a blue streak in French, in English, then in a combination of the two. He glared at the door with fire in his eyes.

"This had better be one hell of an emergency!"

Scraping her composure back together, Danielle took a deep breath and pushed the door open, her eyes rounding as she looked at the person standing behind Dahlia Beauvais. Dahlia was looking a little stunned herself as she said, "Mr. Remy, your voodoo priestess is here."

"Voodoo priestess?" Danielle said, her disbelieving gaze darting from the strange woman to Remy.

"Mam'selle Annick," the young woman said, giving Danielle a dramatic bow, holding her slender arms out to the sides and shaking the array of primitive rattles she held in her hands. She wore a multicolored caftan, belted at her tiny waist with about twenty strands of beads. Around her neck were enough necklaces to put Mr. T to shame. She had a ring on every finger and long red false nails. Her makeup looked like something from *Cats*—outrageously outlined dark eyes, overdone brows, long false lashes. Her black hair had been teased into a lion's mane that stood out all around her head.

Remy didn't seem surprised in the least. He scowled at his visitor and said, "Your timin' stinks."

Mademoiselle Annick's eyes twinkled. The corners of her purple-painted mouth twitched a bit. Danielle had the very disconcerting feeling that the woman knew exactly what she had interrupted. She forced the thought away and turned to Remy with her hands on her hips.

"What's this all about? I'll tell you right now, I'm not letting her put a curse on Jeremy—"

Remy shook a finger at her. "You're startin' to like those kids."

Danielle's nose lifted a fraction. "Don't try to distract me with insults. I know he probably deserves worse than anything Vampira here can dish out, but—"

"Don't worry, *chère*," Remy said, leading her out of the darkroom by the elbow. His temper evaporated entirely as he speculated on what was about to happen. "The mam'selle is here to cure your Mr. Butler."

Danielle frowned. "He isn't going to like this."

"That's what I'm countin' on," Remy muttered under his breath. He'd had enough of that old fraud skulking around spying on him and clicking his tongue in reproach at the way Remy dealt with the duties of his station. But mostly he wanted revenge for the interruption in the kitchen. If it hadn't been for the Scot's meddling, Remy was certain Danielle wouldn't have spent the last three days hiding behind her Nikon and he wouldn't have spent the last three nights under the spray of a cold shower.

They made their way back to Butler's quarters, an odd parade with Danielle and Remy leading the way, followed by the bizarre Mam'selle Annick, and trailed by the Beauvais children all bursting with curiosity. Remy flung the door back without knocking. Butler jumped then bent over the putter he'd been practicing with and hobbled across the room to his bed, using the golf club like a cane.

"Time for your medicine, old friend," Remy said with a smirk.

"Butler!" Danielle exclaimed, stomping across the room. "What are you doing out of bed? Your back is never going to heal properly unless you rest it."

Butler flushed guiltily and dodged her gaze. "Just changing the telly," he mumbled, settling back against the pillows.

"There's a remote control for that."

He snorted and waved a hand. "I canna work the blasted thing. Too many wee buttons."

Danielle gave him a doubtful look. Her father's house had more electronic gadgets in it than a James Bond movie. Unless the old man was getting senile? Her heart sank horribly at the thought of her old Butler going dotty.

Remy rolled his eyes and pulled his priestess into the room, closing the door in the face of their would-be audience. "No need for those useless pills anymore, Mr. Butler," he said with a jovial grin as he ushered Annick toward the bed. "I've got just the thing here for you. Mam'selle Annick, practitioner of the ancient ways, doctor of roots and fruits. She'll fix you right up *bon*."

Annick shot her brother a glance and spoke softly through her teeth so only he could hear. "Giselle will skin us alive if she finds out about this."

He gave her a look brimming with menace. "Then she'd better not find out, *'tite soeur*."

Butler took one look at the startling mam'selle and blanched. Annick rushed up to the side of the bed, gave him a wild-eyed stare, and shook her rattles at him. The old butler snatched up his putter and warded her off as if with the sword of righteousness. "Ye'll not lay one heathen hand on me, witch!"

Danielle watched with growing suspicion as Annick danced around in a circle chanting the words to "Iko, Iko," the old Dixie Cups song, shaking her rattles. Then she tossed some brown powder at him that smelled suspiciously like instant hot cocoa. At the foot of the bed Remy stood with his arms crossed over his chest, fighting a furious battle with laughter, his mustache twitching.

His face red with an oncoming attack of apoplexy, Butler took a poke at the priestess with the golf club. "Be off with ye, heathen wench! I'll have none of your dark ways practiced in this house!" He stole a glance at Danielle and suddenly fell back against his pillows with a pained expression. "Ooooh! I've taxed it again! 'Tis all his fault!" he wailed, pointing an accusatory putter at Remy.

Remy started to protest but was cut off by a dark look from Danielle.

"Okay, folks, the floor show's over," she said dryly, catching hold of the dancing priestess by one of her bead belts, nearly toppling her. She escorted the woman to the door and shooed her out, scattering wide-eyed Beauvaises in every direction. "Send your bill in care of Mr. Doucet," Danielle said with a smile. "And if he doesn't pay promptly, feel free to create a likeness of him and stick it full of pins."

Closing the door in the priestess's face, Danielle turned and regarded Remy with a dire look. "You ought to be ashamed of yourself, perpetrating such a hoax."

"Me?" Remy itched to denounce his adversary. He scowled at Butler, who was looking altogether too smug, and ground his teeth. He couldn't expose the Scot or the Scot would expose him. He couldn't tell Danielle her precious old butler was playing her for a sucker without having her find out that he himself had duped her as well.

"I think you have some apologizing to do, Mr. Doucet," Danielle said primly. "I'll leave you to it."

Remy seethed as Danielle let herself out of the room. He whirled around to shake a finger at Butler. "You're a fraud, old man."

"So are you," Butler volleyed, a truculent gleam in his eye and his putter at the ready.

"Your back isn't any worse than mine."

"And you're no more a nanny than my big toe."

"Seems to me what we've got us here is a good old-fashioned Mexican standoff, Scottie," Remy said, deftly plucking away Butler's putter. He nudged a couple of golf balls out from under the bed skirt with his toe, took a practiced stance, and methodically tapped each across the rug. The first missed its mark by a fraction of an inch. The second rolled precisely into the overturned water glass tucked beneath the armoire. Holding his position, he glanced over at Butler and raised a brow. "What are we gonna do about this, *mon ami*?"

Butler narrowed his shrewd blue eyes, taking in both Remy's face and his grip on the golf club. He seemed to consider for a moment. "You're a golfing man, Mr. Do-sit?"

"Had a nine handicap back in my oil company days."

He nodded and his expression softened a bit, as if Remy's impressive handicap automatically qualified him as a decent sort of person. Finally he tugged close the belt of his plaid robe and said, "I'll no have ye hurt the lass."

"I don't plan on hurting her. Seems to me she's been hurting herself enough, yes?"

"Oh, aye, laddie," Butler murmured. He compressed his mouth briefly, as if warding off an inner pain that had nothing to do with his back. "She has that. She has indeed."

Remy pulled a chair up alongside the bed and settled himself in it, propping his feet up on the mattress. Still playing absently with the putter, he gave Butler a long level look and said, "Why don't you tell ol' Remy all about it?"

Butler stared back at him, outwardly impassive, inwardly pleased.

"It's me," he whispered into the receiver after Remy had gone. "Not to worry. Everything is back on track. Better than ever. Oh, aye, we hit a wee bit of a snag there for a day or two, but it's all coming around. It'll all work out in the end, I'm sure of it."

# Nine

Switching off the lights in the darkroom, Danielle let herself out into the hall. She had seen neither Remy nor Butler since the Mam'selle Annick freak-show incident earlier in the evening. She wondered if they had settled their differences. Butler had wasted no opportunity to defame Remy's name to her every chance he'd had over the past few days. And Remy's opinion of Butler was not by any means glowing. The whole thing smacked of jealousy. She smiled a little at the thought, but quickly forced the corners of her mouth back down.

The nursery door stood open and she walked toward it automatically, resigned to taking up her nightly vigil. Her own bed would bring nothing but nightmares.

Remy sat in the rocker, moving it slightly to and fro. His hair was tousled, gleaming faintly in the pale light. He wore the same unbuttoned white oxford shirt he had the first night. His unlit cigarette dangled from his lip. Snuggled into the crook of his brawny arm was the baby, sleeping peacefully as Remy sang to her in a whisper-soft voice.

Danielle knew she should turn and run. Her instincts were telling her to get far away as fast as she could. But she couldn't move. She was rooted to the spot and the scene before her worked its magic with a swiftness that took her breath away.

What could have looked more precious, more loving, than the sight of a big tough macho guy like Remy Doucet holding a baby in fuzzy pajamas? He was the picture of raw virility, yet he held Eudora with such care, such tenderness. And his voice, so low and rough, was as soft as eiderdown as he sang to her in the language he knew first and best.

He looked up at her and she knew it was too late to back out.

"That was lovely," she whispered, taking another hesitant step toward him. "What was it about?"

"A guy who gets steamed at his pal for raidin' his trotlines. They beat each other senseless then go off together to drink and complain about the cruelty of women."

"Charming."

"It's my brother's favorite."

"He must be quite a guy."

Remy thought about it and decided to reserve comment. He loved his brother Etienne, nicknamed Lucky. Lucky's reputation with women was notorious, however, and every girl in Partout Parish had been in love with him at one time or another. Lucky, of course, had never let any woman steal his heart or his freedom, but that had only spurred the feminine instinct to domesticate him. It was a strange phenomenon and not one Remy cared to test with Danielle. He planned to keep her all to himself.

His little heart-to-heart with Butler had been enlightening. He wondered now how much he should let Danielle know he knew. He certainly wouldn't tell her about the little alliance he and the old man had formed. At best she'd have their hides if she found out about that. As for the rest, he decided he should play it by ear.

"I was heading for bed," Danielle said. "Thought I'd take a peek in here first."

"Mmm."

She glanced at the baby. "I can see she's fine, so . . ."

She looked even more hesitant about leaving the room than coming in. Remy's heart twisted with sympathy for her. She would have denied it with her last breath, but she was afraid to leave the baby. Remy had sensed that the first night. He'd sensed it every time he had come to check on the baby and had found Danielle sitting in the very chair he sat in now, keeping a silent vigil over her niece. He hadn't intruded those nights. He had simply watched her from the covering darkness of the hall. Now he knew Danielle's secret. Even if he hadn't known, he had seen the fear in her eyes. He had sensed the conflict within her that tore at her soul every night.

Rising carefully out of the rocker, he leaned over the crib and settled Eudora in among her stuffed toys and teething rings, then covered her with a light blanket. When he turned Danielle's gaze darted from the baby to him and back again.

"Maybe I'll sit here for a while and unwind," she said, her voice nowhere near as confident as she would have liked.

She took a step toward the rocking chair but Remy turned and caught her shoulders gently with his big hands. She looked at him sharply, unable to decide how she should interpret or reply to his actions.

"She's fine, Danielle," he murmured. "She's just asleep."

"I know that," Danielle said defensively. Her gaze

belied her words, though, darting to the child, intent upon seeing the baby's chest rise and fall.

Aching for her, Remy pulled her into his embrace. He wrapped his arms around her and rubbed his cheek against her mane of silvery waves. "It wasn't your fault, darlin'," he whispered.

He knew. Danielle didn't bother to pretend ignorance. Remy knew about London, about Ann Fielding's baby. Apparently he and Butler had more than buried the hatchet, she thought wryly, feeling betrayed and vulnerable.

"It wasn't your fault," he said again.

Danielle disconnected herself from his embrace, shrugging off the comfort he offered because she didn't believe she deserved it. "Tell that to the woman whose baby died while I was supposed to be watching."

"It wouldn't have made a damn bit of difference if you'd been standing right there."

"Well, I wasn't standing right there," she said bitterly, the old recrimination coming easily to the surface. "I was in my darkroom engrossed in the only thing I do very well or care about at all. I was working instead of watching my friend's baby the way I had promised I would. I was so engrossed in printing my latest masterpiece that I completely forgot Ann's daughter was asleep in the next room. By the time Ann came back her baby was dead."

"Sudden infant death," Remy said, nodding. Butler had explained. Remy had some knowledge about the syndrome from reading Giselle's child-rearing periodicals while he'd been tending the phone at the agency. He knew enough not to condemn the woman before him. "You couldn't have prevented it, Danielle. No one could have."

"I could have been there," she whispered, her voice choked with remembered pain and regret.

She would have given anything, anything in the

world, to relive that night. She would have given her talent if she could have. Tears spilled down her cheeks now as she realized, not for the first time, that nothing she could do now would make amends. No amount of pain, no amount of self-sacrifice, would bring Ann's baby back.

She brought a fist to her mouth and bit down hard on one knuckle as she thought of the tiny life that had slipped away that night, all alone in the darkness of a strange room, with no familiar voice or touch to say good-bye. And the pain sliced her heart in two as if a year hadn't passed, as if enough years could never pass to dull it.

Her shoulders shook convulsively as the sobs wracked her—silent because she didn't want to share them. Still, when Remy turned her and put his arms around her, she didn't fight him. She didn't have the strength. The pain was hers alone to bear, but God help her, she didn't have the strength to turn away his second offer of comfort. It was just another weakness in her. What was one more?

She let her head fall to the broad width of his shoulder. She let him hold her close and kiss her hair. She let herself cry. In her mind she made herself listen again to Ann's bitter accusations. Danielle was not fit to be around children, she had screamed. Danielle was disgustingly selfish and consumed by her work. Danielle was a woman who never deserved to be a mother. And Danielle cried harder because she knew it was all true.

"Don't cry so, darlin'," Remy whispered around the lump in his throat. "Don't cry so, *chère*, you're breakin' my heart."

He hurt so for her, he nearly couldn't stand it. Strong, independent Danielle. Danielle, who professed to need no ties. She was trembling in his arms as if the very last ounce of her inner strength was being wrung from her.

"Now you see why I don't belong here," she murmured. "She never should have asked."

"No," Remy said, holding her tighter. "Now I see exactly why she asked." He could also see how deeply Suzannah Beauvais cared for her half-sister and how that love was returned. That Danielle would put herself through such emotional hell just because Suzannah had asked her told him a lot. "She asked because she trusts you."

"Trusted me to hire you, maybe," Danielle conceded. "More likely I was the only person in the western hemisphere who hadn't heard the legend of the Big Bad Beauvais clan. She probably thinks these kids are tough enough to survive anything—even me."

Her voice tightened painfully on those last two words and Remy winced a bit. The lady was hard on herself; not the mark of someone who was habitually selfish. She was unsure of herself; not the sign of a woman so self-possessed that she needed no one else in her life.

"How long are you gonna go on blamin' yourself for somethin' you didn't do?" he asked quietly. "You're only human, Danielle, not God. That baby dyin' was a sad, sad thing, but you didn't cause it. It's somethin' that happens. We don't know why. We can do our grieving, then get on with our lives."

"How can Ann get on with her life? She lost her child."

"And I can't even imagine her pain. But what good will it be for her to let it go on forever? Then two lives are lost, not one, you see. Where is the sense in that? Don't throw your life away, too, Danielle. It won't bring that baby back. You let the guilt drive you away from your family, away from your art, maybe even from me, yes?"

"No!" she said, realizing too late that she was neatly trapped. If she was denying only the last of the statement, then she was admitting that the first part was true. If she thought she was denying the whole charge, then he would know that she was lying. She had banished herself to Tibet to take pictures of bleakness. She had cut people out of her life, thinking to save them from her selfishness. And nothing she had done had made any difference.

He had her dead to rights. The man was too blasted insightful. Since when had men become insightful? Wasn't that against the rules of machismo? Glancing up at Remy, she almost laughed. There hadn't been a rule made this rogue wouldn't go over, under, or around.

"You're a weasel," she said.

"I'm your friend."

That was true, she thought, a little amazed.

Remy smiled gently. "So you gonna stop taking pictures of closed doors and start livin' again, *chère*? Let some of those doors open?"

"Where did you get to be so smart?" she asked dryly, trying to keep herself from bursting into tears of gratitude. "Nanny school?"

Remy bit back his grimace of guilt. This didn't seem the time for a confession that would brand him a fraud. "Just runs in the family, I guess."

"Well, wherever it comes from," she whispered hoarsely, "thanks."

Remy lowered his head and nuzzled her cheek, coaxing her to turn her lips to meet his. She kissed him, her arms sliding up around his neck, her body still pressed limply to his. He had been her anchor as the storm of her emotions had battered her. Now she clung to him still, too spent to let go of his strength. She allowed him to kiss her deeply and thoroughly, but when the kiss was finished she peeled herself away from him and stepped back.

"We shouldn't."

There wasn't much conviction in her voice, Remy

noted. His conscience pointed out to him that only a scoundrel would take advantage of her vulnerability. The little devil on his shoulder rationalized that what Danielle needed was a diversion from her emotional self-flagellation. She needed some fun, some re-nowned Doucet-brand T.L.C. She needed to get in-volved again with life and with people. She might as well start by getting involved with him.

"Why shouldn't we?" he said, his gaze full of chal-lenge. "We're both adults. We know what we want. Hell, sugar, let's be honest. We've both wanted it since the minute you opened that front door and found me on the other side."

Danielle felt the undeniable tingle of temptation as she looked at him. He was impossibly sexy. His shirt hung open, draping down from massive shoulders to frame a thick chest. A carpet of black curls over sculptured muscle thinned at his washboard belly and disappeared into the low-riding waistband of his jeans. But more than this breathtaking masculine vision, she was attracted most by his expression—teasing and tender, sweet and mischievous. The look in his dark eyes invited her to run wild with him, to give in to temptation, to indulge the desires she had been trying for days to repress. She felt more alive just looking at him. The sexual energy rolled off him in waves and heightened her awareness both of him and of her own long-neglected needs.

"There are a million reasons we shouldn't," she said, praying he wouldn't ask her to name them.

With a sexy swagger he closed the distance she had put between them. That devilish light was dancing in his eyes. His mustache twitched up at the corners in a smile reminiscent of a cat closing in on a cornered canary. "All of them together don't add up to a flea."

He put his hands on her shoulders then slid them deliberately down her sides and around to the small of her back, his thumbs brushing the sides of her breasts as they went. He drew her lower body close to his and began swaying as if in time to some sensuous music only he could hear. "Come on, *chère*, admit it, this attraction is bigger than both of us. Why fight it? This is N'Awlins, *bébé*, let the good times roll."

Danielle's hips had begun to move in time with Remy's. She couldn't seem to stop them. Did she really want to? With him so close, so sexy, inciting her senses to riot, her reasons for not getting involved with him drifted away like smoke. It was remarkable, really, how swiftly and effortlessly he had altered her mood.

She quirked a brow at him. "I ought to roll you right out to the unemployment line."

"We'd both have a lot more fun if you'd roll me to your bedroom," he said, bending down to nip at her earlobe. "We can both do some real rollin' then, *oui*?"

Danielle's head swam a little at the images that sprang to mind. He was right. Why was she fighting it? She should have been jumping at the chance to have a fling with an incredibly handsome young stud before she was too old and decrepit to enjoy it. Where was the harm? They would be together for a matter of days. What could possibly go wrong in so short a time?

Somewhere in the dim recesses of her mind she knew the something that could go very wrong. She could fall in love with him. But in her current state of mind she dismissed the possibility. She was a Hamilton; relationships never lasted for her. She knew better than to let her heart get too involved. They would enjoy each other, then go their separate ways with fond memories.

Remy knew the instant she decided in his favor. He felt the wall of her resistance crumble. She stopped dancing and looked up at him, her gray eyes clear and earnest in the pale light of the fading moon. He went still and looked down at her, his heart pounding in his chest, suddenly aware of how much this meant to him. He wanted to take away the tension that had painted dark crescents beneath her eyes. He wanted to show her with his body how desirable she was. He wanted to love all the loneliness out of her restless heart and fill it up with passion.

Without a word he took her hand and led her from the room, stopping only to reassure Danielle that the baby was sleeping peacefully. Sliding an arm around her waist, he guided Danielle down the hall to her room. Her step faltered a bit as he bypassed the bed, but she followed him willingly into the spacious bath where moonlight coming through the window gave the white tile a silver glow.

He didn't turn on a light but went to the long marble vanity and lit the three fat fragrant candles that sat on one end. Their light reflected in the mirror and created a lush pool of amber that extended to the shower stall, which was walled by frosted glass on two sides.

Danielle's knees trembled and her insides turned warm and syrupy at the memory of the day they had met when she had first pictured them together under the hot spray of the shower. The reality was at hand. Remy adjusted the faucets in the stall and by the time he turned toward her steam was already beginning to rise, lending their surroundings an ethereal, mystical quality.

He faced her and slowly shrugged the white shirt from his shoulders, letting it fall to the tile floor. Danielle didn't try to resist the urge to touch him. She raised her hands to his chest and splayed her fingers wide as if to touch as much of him in one stroke as possible. His nostrils flared as she drew her fingertips downward, tracing every ridge and valley of muscle, skimming his rib cage and catching in the waistband of his jeans. He sucked in a breath through his teeth as she teased him, slowly dragging her fingers along just inside his pants to the button. Holding his gaze, she released the metal disk from the buttonhole and traced the newly revealed skin. As she lowered his zipper, he hooked his thumbs in the waist of both jeans and briefs and was out of them in two smooth steps.

He stood back then a little, letting Danielle look her fill. Her mouth went dry at the sight of him magnificently naked in the flickering candlelight. He looked a little primitive and all male, his body a solid block of muscle sculpted by nature into a masterpiece— upper body a powerful wedge, hips trim, thighs sturdy, and at the juncture of those thighs thickening evidence of his desire for her. He grew hard as she watched and the word "magnificent" suddenly took on a whole new meaning for her.

He was easily the most beautiful man she'd ever seen. She made that judgment with the objectivity of an artist. The woman in her agreed wholeheartedly. The woman in her longed to touch, to taste, to experience. She stepped forward. He stepped back, shaking his dark head, a lazy smile carving out the dimple in his cheek.

"Your turn, angel," he murmured. "I like to look too."

Danielle's fingers trembled as she fumbled with the fastening of her shorts. Every insecurity she had about her age came rushing to the surface, but there was no turning back now. She hesitated, glancing up at Remy with a narrow-eyed glare.

"One crack about cellulite and you're a dead man."

Remy's heart melted. If the lady had any idea how much he already loved her, she'd have run like hell. Danielle wasn't ready to hear professions of love. He knew without asking that she thought this would be a short-term affair. He had every intention of proving her wrong, but no intention of tipping his hand at this point.

He moved closer and reached out to cover her hands with his own. Pushing downward, he whispered, "You don't have any idea how beautiful you are, how hot you make me." The shorts dropped to the floor. "How I've dreamed every night about seein' you naked, about touchin' you." He released her right hand and touched her through her panties, sliding his fingers slowly between her legs and rubbing the silk against the tender flesh that was already hot and moist. His voice dropped another rough note. "About havin' you touch me."

Still massaging her with one hand, he drew her hand to his erection and hissed through his teeth as her cool fingers closed around him. His chest rose and fell like bellows as she explored him, stroking the rigid length of him, fingering the velvety tip.

"Oh, Remy," she whispered, her breath shuddering out of her. She felt vaguely faint at the prospect of joining with him. She felt too dizzy to finish undressing herself and decided instead to indulge one of her own fantasies. Looking up at him, her eyes hooded with passion she murmured, "Take off my blouse."

Remy thanked heaven Danielle was wearing a T-shirt and nothing with buttons, because he would have died of frustration getting her out of it. His hands shook violently as he pulled the top up and over her head and flung it aside. All thought of just looking was vaporized as his hungry gaze swept over her body. Her breasts were high and firm, small enough that she could get away without wearing a bra, full enough to make a man's hands itch to touch them—which Remy did not hesitate to do.

He cupped her breasts, one in each hand, and brushed his thumbs over her dark nipples, wringing a gasp from her. The gasp turned to a groan as he quickly bent his head and took first one rigid peak and then the other into his mouth for a hard sucking kiss. His hands swept down over her then, as he returned his mouth hungrily to hers. Tongues dueled and teeth clashed and he hooked his thumbs in the waistband of her panties and jerked them down, pulling her up and against him in his next move, his fingers biting into the soft flesh of her buttocks.

Danielle moaned at the feel of his maleness, hard and hot between them, pressing urgently into the smoothness of her belly as his tongue thrust aggressively into her mouth. She wrapped her arms around the small of his back and slid her hands down over the deliciously rounded swell of his buttocks, squeezing and kneading. Her right knee pulled upward as they kissed and rubbed sensuously against the outer part of his thigh, climbing higher with each stroke of his tongue.

He carried her into the shower, breaking their kiss only long enough to open the glass door to the stall. Danielle wasn't at all sure the steam rising around them wasn't generated by their passion rather than the hot water raining down out of the showerhead. She'd never felt so consumed by the inner flames of desire as she did now. And Remy made his feelings more than clear. He wanted her with an intensity that glittered fiercely in his eyes. All the teasing, the mischief, was gone now, replaced by a rapacious desire that made Danielle's blood sing in her veins.

The water pounded down over them, slicking their skin, adding to the heat. Droplets caught in Remy's chest hair and Danielle collected them with her tongue. He stood for the torture until she flicked a drop off one flat nipple. Then a growl rumbled low in his throat and he hauled her up against him for another kiss.

Backing her into a wall covered in smooth tile, he lifted her with a hand on the back of each thigh, tilting her hips toward him. Pulling her legs around his hips, he moaned as he sank into the tight hot pocket of her womanhood. His breath caught in his throat and he whispered to her, urgent words, words of praise, words of sex in a language she didn't speak. The message was plain enough, and Danielle responded by moving against him.

It was wonderful, primal, perfect, she thought. She rejoiced at the feel of him moving inside her and against her, pinning her to the tile. He made love with earthy honesty, holding nothing back. He made her feel more alive than she'd felt in a long, long time. She wanted to tell him so, but there didn't seem to be enough breath in her lungs. Besides, her mouth seemed perfectly happy fused to his, and her brain had other things to think about—like the incredible sensation that was building and building in the pit of her belly. She concentrated on the feeling of it growing and growing with Remy's every thrust, until it burst and she was caught up in the wild whirlwind of the explosion.

She clung to Remy's broad shoulders as he, too, surrendered to a shuddering climax. In the end they were both gasping for breath. Danielle managed a weary smile and coughed.

"I'm drowning," she mumbled.

"Oh . . . me, too, *chère*. That was incredible."

"No, I mean—" She coughed again. "I'm really drowning."

"Huh?" He raised his head from her shoulder and his eyes widened as he realized the spray of the shower was hitting her full force in the face. "Oh, jeeze. I'm sorry, darlin'."

"It's okay," she said. He slid out of her but held her close still. They leaned against each other as if for support. Danielle wound her arms around his waist. "What a way to go."

Remy picked up the thick bar of imported soap and began running it up and down her back, smiling as she arched against his touch like a cat. His hands brushed the suds down over her hips to her delightfully rounded derriere and he shook his head slightly at her insecurity about her looks. She had a body a lot of younger women would have wanted. A lot of men, too, he thought, a surge of jealousy burning through him. Danielle was a very desirable woman. It was his job to prove that to her tonight.

Stepping back, he brought his hands around to the front of her and began the process all over again, slicking bubbles over her breasts, her belly. He lowered his head and kissed her as he teased her mercilessly with the bar of soap, until she was gasping for mercy. Then she managed to wrest the bar away from him and set off to do a little teasing of her own.

They made love again under the spray, then dried each other with thick towels. Remy put the candles out and ushered Danielle from the room, turning on a small table lamp as they returned to her bedroom.

"Will you stay with me?" she asked quietly, feeling suddenly uncertain again. It had been a long time since she'd shared a bed. It had been forever since she'd wanted to as badly as she did now.

He turned her by her shoulders and looked into her eyes, reading secrets in their pewter depths that she couldn't hide from him now, so close after they had shared the ultimate physical intimacy. Love and protectiveness swelled in his heart. He caught her chin in his hand and gave her a fierce, sexy look. "You try to send me away, sugar."

One corner of her mouth tilted up in a shadow of a familiar, wry smile. "I'd rather do the opposite. Wouldn't you?"

Remy chuckled and tumbled her onto the bed, rolling them over until he was on top and he held Danielle's arms pressed to the mattress above her head. Dark eyes glittering, he leaned down and flicked his tongue across her nipple.

"Oh . . . absolutely, darlin'. Absolutely."

# Ten

"Five Beauvais turned loose on an unsuspecting public with only two adults to supervise," Danielle murmured, shuddering involuntarily.

She stood on the side veranda in a black tank top and khaki walking shorts, staring apprehensively at the loaded minivan in the driveway. The older children had already settled into the vehicle after a spirited battle for choice seats. Dahlia was sitting on the far side in the backseat, only her silhouette visible due to the shade of an enormous magnolia tree and the shadow cast by the wide brim of her straw hat. Danielle thought she was being a little too unobtrusive and made a mental note to check for makeup before they pulled out. Ambrose sat at the opposite window wearing a pirate eye patch and a bandana tied around his head. Tinks and Jeremy had commandeered the seats in the far back of the vehicle. At the present moment, however, Jeremy was attempting to lower Tinks to the pavement by her ankles through the opened back window.

"Jeremy, haul your sister back inside and behave

yourself!" Remy called calmly, stepping out the door with Eudora on one arm. On the other hung an umbrella stroller, its handles hooked around his forearm. Over his shoulder was slung a blindingly pink diaper bag. The picture he presented was incongruous and adorable.

"I don't know about this, Remy." Danielle shot him a glance. "Are you sure we can do it?"

Remy's gaze immediately turned hotter than the Louisiana summer. "I suppose we could call off this little field trip, lock ourselves in your room, and spend the day findin' out." His eyelashes swept down like black lace fans. His voice was like liquid smoke. "But after last night, I don't know how you can ask."

Danielle blushed to the roots of her hair. "That's not what I meant!"

He clucked his tongue in reproach. "You gotta stop leadin' me on this way, Danielle."

"Leading you on?" Danielle sputtered, briefly considering smacking him with her camera bag. "I ought to lead you to the unemployment line."

"But you need me," he singsonged.

She pretended a scowl. "I refuse to answer that on the grounds that you will turn it into a sexual innuendo."

"Sexual innuendo." He growled and leaned toward her, his eyelids drooping lazily. "I love the way you say that. It sounds so kinky. Will you whisper it in my ear?"

"I'll box your ear." Danielle fought the giggles that threatened and snatched the baby away from him. "You should be ashamed, saying things like that in front of an impressionable child."

She tried to straighten the impossibly crooked yellow bow she had tied in a strand of Eudora's red hair. The baby squealed a protest and sprayed the front of Danielle's blouse with spittle.

"That'll be an interesting defense mechanism when she's old enough to date," Danielle said, unaffected.

She was in too good a mood to let a little saliva ruin her day. She snatched a towel out of a pouch on the diaper bag and repaired the damage as best she could.

Butler came to the door to see them off. He stooped over and hung onto the brass doorknob for support, going through his repertoire of pained faces. "I'm sorry I canna go with ye, lass," he said, looking properly contrite.

"Me too." Danielle suspiciously eyed the plaid golf slacks peeking out beneath the hem of his robe. "You know, Butler, the walk might do you good."

"Oh, no," Remy blurted out. "Rest and relaxation." He gave her an annoyed glance and started for the van. "The man oughta know his own back, Danielle."

"Wise, wise," Butler chanted, nodding sagely, gazing off after Remy with approval. "And a braw handsome lad too. Och, a lass could do worse."

Danielle gave him a strange look. "Stay out of the sun, Butler. You're not used to all this heat. I think it's affecting you."

They loaded the baby into her car seat, then settled in themselves, Remy behind the wheel. Dahlia was sent back to the house to remove the half-pound of makeup she had worn. Ambrose waited until they were to the end of the driveway to decide he had to go to the bathroom. They had to pull over when Jeremy and Tinks fell on each other in mortal combat over who could spit the farthest. But eventually they made it to the zoo.

The day was hot and clear, the butter-yellow sunshine filtering down through the haze of humidity to which Danielle was gradually becoming accustomed. It was the heart of summer in the Deep South, hot, sultry, semitropical. If her crisp cotton shorts were wilted before they made it through the entry gate, then everyone else around her was wilted too. Except Remy. He didn't look wilted, she thought as she took in his outfit of cuffed black walking shorts that molded his fabulous fanny and a loose white shirt that accented his dark skin. He looked wonderful . . . touchable . . . good enough to eat.

He caught her looking and sent her a secret smile. Danielle felt the now familiar zip of electricity racing through her to curl her toes inside her canvas sneakers. She smiled back, feeling like a giddy teenager with her first big crush on the football captain.

They had made love long into the night, Remy tapping a well of sexuality in her she hadn't known existed. He had slept in her bed till dawn, then crept back to his own room before the children woke. One night in Remy's arms had left her feeling full of life's joy and ready to take on any challenge—even supervising her nieces and nephews at the zoo. The quiet talk she and Remy had shared, both in the nursery and later in bed, had soothed her fears about her abilities to handle and relate to children. He had told her to relax and not worry so much about goofing up on little things, and she had decided to take his advice. He was the expert, after all. Besides, trying a fresh approach was certainly better than being miserable with the status quo.

They strolled the paths together at Remy's stern insistence. Dahlia led the way, staying just enough in front of them so she wouldn't feel embarrassed by being with "kids." Jeremy and Tinks came next. Jeremy in a camouflage cap, Tinks in a plastic pith helmet. Both of them with their eyes peeled for misadventure. Remy pushed Eudora in the stroller. Danielle held hands with Ambrose, who had added a blue Audubon Zoo visor to his pirate getup.

Also there at Remy's insistence was Danielle's trusty Nikon, hanging around her neck like an amulet. He encouraged her to take pictures of everything and, more importantly, everyone. And for the first time in a year she broke her self-imposed ban on photographing people. She photographed the children, the animals, the zookeepers, men in Bermuda shorts and black socks, women who had attempted to squeeze winter-fat bodies into summer spandex outfits. It was like breaking a fast. She started slowly, then made a glutton of herself. By lunchtime she had gone through five rolls of film.

And as they walked along, browsing at flamingos and sea lions and tigers, Danielle let herself fantasize that they were a family, she and Remy and the Beauvais brood—just to see what it would be like. It wasn't that she had any intention of marrying and having five children. Not at all, she assured herself. She was merely a little curious, that was all.

It felt okay.

It felt nice.

*The day was not without its little incidents.*

*Jeremy, leave those snakes alone . . . So sorry, sir. We adopted him from a circus. One can only imagine the kind of upbringing a child receives from clowns.*

*Jeremy, where's Tinks? What do you mean she found a hole in the fence?*

*Sorry, ma'am, I'm sure she didn't realize it was an endangered species.*

*Tinks, where's your brother? . . . What wading pond? . . . The one by the alliga—!*

*It's too bad we missed your sister today,"* Danielle said. "I would have liked to meet her. She must have just missed us.

"Yeah," Remy said with a notable lack of remorse. "What a shame."

He cast a glance heavenward and thanked that little angel he so often ignored. He shuddered to think what kind of shape he'd be in now if it had been Giselle at the darkroom door last night rather than Annick. His conscience pricked him at the reminder of the little secret he was still keeping from Danielle, but he ignored it. There was plenty of time to tell her he wasn't exactly a nanny. Besides, everything was going perfectly as far as he could see. He had more important things on his mind tonight.

"Have you really been to all those places you were tellin' the kids about tonight?" Remy asked.

They were comfortably ensconced on the porch swing, Remy leaning back into the corner with his left foot planted on the bench and his right on the floor. Danielle lay against him, her head on his chest, her long legs tucked up on the seat. The children had all been fed, bathed, and put to bed with the array of stuffed animals Danielle had bought for them in the zoo's gift shop. Butler, looking oddly flushed—almost sunburned, Danielle thought—had eaten dinner with them, but had pleaded a headache the instant Danielle had commented on his appearance, and had retired to his quarters.

The Beauvais house was peaceful. The night was full of the sounds of insects, the distant wail of blues from a house down the block. The air was still thick with humidity and the scent of boxwood and roses, sweet olive and dozens of other plants that flourished in the hothouse environment of the Southern summer. Danielle smiled sleepily, comfortable and happy in the oasis of yellow light on the veranda, comfortable leaning against Remy rather than fighting against the attraction she felt for him.

"Sure," she said, around a lazy yawn. "I've been all around the world."

She said it as if it were the most commonplace thing, as if she thought everybody had been to Malta and Taipei and Antarctica. Remy tired to ignore the stirring of nerves in his belly. Of course it was commonplace to Danielle, he told himself. She had traveled from an early age. It was probably old hat, boring stuff to her by now . . . he hoped. Even as he hoped he heard the echo of an earlier conversation when she'd said she loved discovering new places and meeting new people.

A chill chased over his skin despite the fact that the night was hot. He brought a hand up to toy with the wildly curling tendrils of Danielle's hair. So soft, so silvery. A strand coiled naturally around his index finger and he wished it would be so easy to bind her to him. The light glittered off the bracelets that were draped around her delicate wrist like strands of angel's hair and he wished he could somehow use them to chain together their hearts.

He was in love with her. He wasn't precisely certain when it had happened. It might have been when she had turned to him in tears. It might have been when he'd watched her watch the baby sleep. It might have been when she had patiently listened while Ambrose had explained why his stuffed dog needed to sleep with a night-light on. All he knew for certain was he had looked at her today as they had walked along the paths of the zoo and realized that he had finally, really fallen in love.

It scared the hell out of him. All his life he'd just assumed he would fall for a Louisiana girl, if not Marie Broussard, then someone else who shared his background and his beliefs. Never in a million years would he have expected to fall for a long-legged blond Yankee with a wanderlust that put the great explorers to shame. But in love was exactly what he was, he had no doubts. It didn't matter that he'd known Danielle only a matter of days. It didn't matter that she'd fought the attraction between them. He was a man who trusted his instincts and his instincts told him in no uncertain terms that this was the Big L.

The question was, what was he going to do about it? What would Danielle do about it if he told her? She was so cynical about relationships. How many times had she told him hers never lasted?

"Where you gonna go next?" he asked in a tone flat from a complete lack of enthusiasm for the topic.

Danielle hesitated. As eager as she had been to get away from New Orleans two days ago, she had no answer now. Everything had changed. The situation had changed. Her feelings had changed. *She* had changed. "Uh—I'm not sure." She shifted position so he wouldn't be able to feel her heart pounding and thought, *I'd stay here if you asked me.*

That was silly, of course, she told herself. Why would he ask her to stay? They were having fun together, but they both knew this was only a very temporary arrangement. She was being uncharacteristically fanciful imagining a future with her handsome young lover.

"Ever been to the bayou country?" Remy asked. Hell, what did he have to lose? He was already in over his heart. Maybe if he took Danielle to the muddy banks along the Bayou Noir, she would find a home at last and forget about the allure of all those exotic places her restless heart had taken her.

She turned and looked up at him and his breath caught at the steady searching gaze of her big pewter-colored eyes. "No," she whispered. "Would you take me?"

*"Oui."*

The word was little more than an exhalation of breath as he leaned forward and captured her parted lips with his. Hope welled inside him, pushing out fear for the moment. Then passion swept all of it aside. He wrapped his arms around Danielle and pulled her even tighter against him as he tried to convey his love to her without words.

It was a slow, deep kiss. Danielle drank it in and savored it, thinking it was more intoxicating than the finest wine, more addictive than any drug. She loved the taste of him. She loved the way he kissed. The brush of his mustache against her upper lip sent shivers dancing over her. The feel of him, strong and solid against her, made her feel safe and feminine and cherished. When she was in his arms nothing else mattered.

No sooner had the thought crossed her mind than the baby monitor sitting on the floor crackled. Instantly Danielle stiffened and tried to push herself off Remy, her heart hammering triple time as all manner of horrible scenarios flashed through her mind.

"Hush," he whispered. "Listen."

She tried to swallow her anxiety as Remy reached down and picked up the black box. She watched, her body still tensed and ready to bolt, as he lifted the monitor close to his ear and listened. Slowly a smile curved his mouth and he tipped the monitor to Danielle's ear.

"She's not in trouble," he said, chuckling softly. "She's talkin' in her sleep."

Danielle sagged against him, all strength draining out of her as she listened to the mumbled stream of baby babble. In that instant she thought she'd never heard anything as dear to her ears.

Remy listened some more then set the box back down. "She must have had quite a time today if she's still talkin' about it. What about you, *chère*? What kind of time did you have?"

"I had a wonderful time," Danielle said candidly. She sat up and regarded him with a serious, honest look. "Thank you."

She didn't have to say for what. It was clear to Remy she was thanking him for helping her take the first steps back from her self-imposed sentence of isolation. He had watched her slowly blossom today, filling with glowing energy as she photographed the children discovering the wonders of the zoo, as she made a few discoveries of her own. Having the opportunity to watch that happen was all the thanks he needed.

"You're a beautiful, vital, talented woman, Danielle," he murmured. "The world shouldn't be robbed of you." His mustache quirked up and his dimple dented his cheek. "See, I was the one being selfish, no?"

"No."

Her disagreement elicited nothing more than a Gallic shrug that blithely dismissed the topic. Danielle let the topic slide. There was no point getting maudlin when both of them knew exactly what had happened and why. No matter what the future brought, she would always have a special place in her heart for this man because he had helped her heal a wound that might have ruined her life. She hadn't forgotten what had happened in London. She never would. But it would no longer gnaw at her like a cancer, eating away at her soul, a little bit more each day.

"Well," she said on a sigh, pushing herself off the swing. She stretched like a cat and yawned again. "I guess it's time to call it a day. We should get some rest so we can be ready for whatever diabolical scheme Jeremy has planned for tomorrow."

"You're goin' to bed?"

"I guess," she said, fighting a smile of anticipation. She gave him a long look as electricity crackled in the air between them. "What are you going to do?"

"Me?" Remy got up slowly, making a great show of considering his options. He gave her a bland look that was ruined by the banked fires in his dark eyes. He shuffled a little nearer and a little nearer, until a scant inch of humid air separated them. He traced a finger over the vee of her collarbone. "Me, I thought I might take a *long* shower first."

A feline smile curved Danielle's mouth as she tilted her head and looked at him from under her lashes. "You need any help with that, *cher*?"

# *Eleven*

"I'm gonna go all over the world, just like you do, Auntie Danielle," Jeremy said between slurps of cereal. "I'm gonna go all around finding weird animals and catching them like that guy on *Wild Kingdom*."

Danielle beamed. It seemed she'd finally struck a chord with her little relatives by telling them tales of her travels. She felt ridiculously pleased.

Tinks looked up, a milk mustache on her upper lip. "Yeah, and I'm gonna follow him around and take pictures and we'll go all over to places like Africa and Borneo and get shot at by guys with spears like Indiana Jones."

"I'm gonna be a garbage man," Ambrose announced shyly, his cheeks flushed with secret passion.

The other two snorted their derision, Tinks reaching over to push down the brim of Ambrose's black gaucho hat.

"Leave him alone," Remy snapped. "There's nothin' wrong with bein' a garbage man."

Tinks and Jeremy exchanged another glance, deciding by tacit agreement to make their exit before their nanny's temper boiled over. Danielle watched them slink away, followed by Ambrose. The door swung shut and Danielle looked at Remy. He was scowling down at his bowl with a thunderous expression that had apparently scared the snap, crackle, and pop right out of his cereal.

He raised his eyes to her face. "I was a garbage man during the summers when I was in college. You wanna make somethin' of it?"

"No."

"Well, I didn't traipse all over the ever-lovin' world doin' it. I was right here in N'Awlins the whole time." He scraped his chair back from the table and turned to tend Eudora.

So that was what this turn toward churlishness was all about. Danielle raised her eyebrows. Remy had been in a strange mood for two days—ever since their trip to the zoo. In that time Jeremy and Tinks had not stopped pumping her for stories about the exotic places she'd been. She had indulged them enthusiastically, never thinking that Remy might feel left out as she had felt left out many times before. He had managed to shed his temper in time for his midnight visits to her room, but she had to admit his lovemaking had taken on a certain fierceness. Not violence, just a certain edge, as if he were trying to convince her of something.

He had convinced her that he was incredible in bed. She flushed at the thought. He'd taken her places she hadn't dreamed existed. They'd done things she'd only read about in books. It was heady stuff, the intensity of his passion. It made her giddy just thinking about it. It was silly. It was wonderful. It was more than she'd thought she could hope for. It was . . . love.

Oh, no, she thought, pressing a hand to her forehead as if to feel for a fever. It couldn't be love.

She was mistaken. She couldn't have fallen in love with him.

She glanced across the room with a kind of desperation, her gaze fastening on Remy as he attempted to hose oatmeal off Eudora with the spray nozzle on the kitchen sink. Her heart rolled over like a trained poodle.

Remy turned, the baby tucked under his arm like a baton. He draped a dish towel over her head and rubbed at her hair. *"Mon Dieu, chère,"* he said, taking in Danielle's stricken expression. "You look like you got a whiff of the diaper pail. What's wrong?"

"Wrong?" *Oh, nothing. I'm just making a fool of myself, that's all.*

"Look, sugar, I'm sorry I snapped at you. I was worried you might think less of me 'cause I was a garbage man." It was part of the truth, anyway, Remy thought. He was feeling a little too vulnerable to tell her what was really bothering him, namely her attraction to travel. He had tried leaving Louisiana once and had given up his career in order to come back. The thought of leaving again made his heart sink, but the idea of Danielle leaving him behind had much the same effect. Unless he could convince her to stay, it was a no-win situation.

"You were a garbage man in New Orleans in the summer. I think you deserve a medal," she said. "I might have an obscene amount of money in my bank account, but that doesn't make me a snob, you know."

He worked up a wily grin as he took his seat. "How obscene?" He leaned across the corner of the table, staring at her mouth. "Will you whisper it in my ear tonight?"

Danielle rolled her eyes, ignoring the bolt of desire that rammed through her. She watched as Remy perched Eudora on his knee and played peek-a-boo with her with the dish towel. "Are you really supposed to wash babies with the dish sprayer that way?"

"Oh, yeah, absolutely. It's much better than the bathtub."

"Hmm . . . I think you really started something with Jeremy. His sudden interest in zoology is great. Before that trip to the zoo all he ever talked about was living in a secret tunnel in the sewer and robbing banks. You may have gotten him off *America's Most Wanted* and onto *Wild Kingdom*."

"Hard to picture, huh?"

"Yeah. Well, I guess I've pictured him on *Wild Kingdom*, but not in the Jim Fowler role. I can hear Marlin Perkins saying, 'While I repair the tent flap Jim is downstream struggling to subdue Jeremy, the Wild Boy of the Garden District.'"

Remy chuckled, "You're startin' to like that boy."

"I'm sure I'll get over it."

*I hope not, sugar*, Remy thought, *I'm betting my heart on it.*

They drove out into the bayou country packed into the minivan like sardines. Going west out of New Orleans they encountered swamps and marshlands as the city faded behind them. The landscape changed to chemical factories with smokestacks thrusting into the sky like rusty exclamation marks. Then came rice paddies and canebrakes and sugarcane processing plants. Miles of elevated highway seemed to float above endless acres of undulating saw grass. Glimpses of bayous spread back into the cypress stands like ink spots. Danielle watched it all roll past with the same kind of wonder she experienced seeing any new place for the first time, her eyes automatically assessing everything she saw for its possible artistic value.

Remy watched her out of the corner of his eye as he

drove, taking them off the interstate and into the region of Louisiana known as Acadiana. More than once he realized he was holding his breath, waiting for an adverse reaction. It was terrible how badly he wanted her to like his home country. The potential for disappointment was enormous. He was leaving himself wide open for a broken heart, but then he guessed love wasn't worth much if there wasn't this heightened sense of awareness and fear. It made him feel acutely alive, acutely aware of every nerve ending just under his skin. He kept the Cajun station on the radio turned down to a whisper and still it seemed loud to him as he held his breath and waited for Danielle's verdict.

Suddenly she looked over at him and smiled her wide brilliant smile and said softly, "It's beautiful, Remy." And he felt the dam of tension burst inside him and relief flood through him to the very tips of his fingers and toes.

Luck, Louisiana, ranked just above "wide spot in the road" on Danielle's scale of town sizes. Luck had not one but two traffic lights, although one seemed more than sufficient. The main street boasted the usual small-town businesses. There was a grocery store with a sign in the window advertising a special on crawfish and a butcher shop with a sign in the window saying *"Ici on parle français,"* indicating that French was the language of choice inside.

Luck was shabby and quaint in the way of small towns everywhere, and Danielle fell in love with it on the spot. Her hands itched to pick up her camera and capture it all on film—the restaurant advertising cold Dixie beer and boudin sausage, the thin old men sitting on a bench in front of the hardware store swapping tales of times gone by and watching diligently for strangers, the woman emerging from Yvette's Salon with a fresh permanent.

They drove into a residential area and skipped over a couple of blocks until they found the street that ran parallel to the Bayou Noir, a wide ribbon of sluggish water that was as black as its name promised. The last house along the row of neat bungalows set well back from the bayou belonged to Remy's parents. It was a pretty brick ranch-style house with a screened porch running along the entire front. It was shaded by live oak hung with bunting of gray moss and there was a little flower shrine with a white statue of the Virgin Mary in the middle of the front yard.

Noelle Doucet came out a side door wiping her hands on her apron. She greeted them all with smiles and hugs as if they were relatives who had been too long away from her. She was a small plump woman with sparkling dark eyes. The scent of baking bread clung to her like perfume. She welcomed her son home with a kiss and a rapid stream of French.

"Where's Papa?" he asked.

"Down at Lawrence's gettin' a part for his motor. He'll be back in time for supper. He's never late for a meal, that man." She smiled at Danielle in feminine conspiracy. "Late for his own wedding, yes. Late for supper, *mais non!*"

Remy engulfed her in a big bear hug that had her giggling like a girl of twenty. Danielle looked on, enjoying the sight but feeling a faint twinge at the same time. He looked so young—a grown-up boy teasing his mother, his eyes shining with a distinctive resemblance to Noelle's. "What's for supper, *Maman*?" he asked. "You cookin' my favorites?"

"My gumbo and maquechou and bread puddin' for dessert if you behave yourself, *cher.*"

"I guess that means there'll be plenty for the rest of us," Danielle said dryly.

Noelle laughed and disentangled herself from her son's embrace, saying something to him in French that made him blush.

"She's wondering if I've finally brought home a prospective daughter-in-law," Remy whispered to Danielle as his mother busied herself getting acquainted with Butler and the Beauvais children.

Danielle went utterly still, staring up at Remy without the usual snappy rejoinder. Her cheeks grew hot and she cursed her adolescent reaction.

Remy's gaze burned a smoldering shade darker as he studied her. "You're blushin', angel," he murmured, feeling a little flushed himself at the implications of her silence.

"That's not a blush, it's a hot flash," she grumbled. "Early sign of menopause."

Remy chuckled and brushed a kiss to her temple.

"We're going to be a huge imposition on your parents, Remy." The house looked a comfortable size, but it didn't seem big enough to hold them all. Danielle shuddered to think of turning her nieces and nephews loose in someone else's home. God only knew the havoc they would wreak.

"We aren't stayin' here. We'll be at the Hotel Doucet," he said, hooking a thumb in the direction of the bayou.

Danielle squinted against the sun as she looked west. "That looks like a barge."

"You got it in one, *chère.*"

They walked over to explore the accommodations, leaving Noelle in her glory serving cookies and lemonade to the children at the picnic table in the backyard. Butler watched Eudora as he sprawled in a chaise on the patio; he waved them off with a placid smile.

"He's certainly changed his tune about you," Danielle said as they crunched down the clamshell path toward the barge.

A secret smile tugged up the corner of Remy's mustache as he thought of the alliance he and the Scot had formed. Once Remy had made it clear he cared deeply for Danielle the irascible old butler had been the picture of cooperation. "Guess he just had to get to know me. To know me is to love me," he said, grinning and batting his thick eyelashes at her.

Wasn't that the truth, Danielle thought, her heart jolting in her chest. She had gotten to know him, had fallen in love with him, and now she was in over her head. It was yet to be determined whether she would sink or swim.

The Hotel Doucet, as Remy called it, was a camp-boat, a wood-frame house built on the rusting hull of a barge. It had originally belonged to Remy's grand-parents, but now served as guest house for visiting relatives when the main house overflowed. The house itself was two stories high and one room wide, the exterior covered in gray cypress shakes. Big sections of the first-floor walls were hinged, raised and propped up on railroad ties, creating a gallery of sorts and revealing huge screens that would let the evening breeze through but keep the insects out.

Much of the deck of the barge had been covered in vibrant green AstroTurf. Halved whiskey barrels squatted in strategic spots, overflowing with gerani-ums and petunias. A concrete turtle peeked out from under a huge hairy fern. A cherub balanced a bird-bath on one pudgy shoulder. The overall effect was a little like a miniature golf course, but homey and welcoming.

Danielle was delighted. "The kids will love staying here!"

"Yeah, I don't know about you and me, though. It's kinda small." He gave her a long, somber, meaningful look. "We aren't gonna have any . . . privacy."

"Oh."

Her look of disappointment warmed him. He slung an arm around her shoulders and walked her to the bow of the barge. "I know you're sad, sugar, but don't pout. You can live without me for a couple of nights."

Danielle ducked away from him, shooting him a

look. "Yeah, I've lived thirty-nine years, three hundred and sixty some nights without you. I think I can manage a couple more."

Remy snatched hold of her hands, pulled her to him, and danced her around the deck, grinning like a pirate. "That wasn't what you were sayin' last night, *chère*."

"Oh! Not fair! The words of a woman on the brink of orgasm cannot be held against her."

"No? Can I be held against her?"

Without waiting for an answer he pulled her into his arms and kissed her soundly. They had danced around to the far side of the house and were out of sight from the road. For the moment it was just the two of them with only a spindle-legged heron watching them from the far side of the bayou. Remy pressed his palms against her back, splaying his fingers wide. His mouth slanted against Danielle's temptingly, insistently, his tongue seeking and gaining entrance to the honeyed warmth beyond her lips.

Gulping air, he changed angles and kissed her again. His right hand strayed down the curve of her hip then up again to find her breast and fondle her budding nipple, and he smiled and caught her sigh of pleasure with his mouth.

"I've arranged for us to have a little time alone tomorrow," he murmured against her lips. "I want to give you a tour . . . among other things."

Danielle lifted her sleepy lids and tried to clear her head of the sensual haze Remy had so easily stirred up. "What about the kids?"

"Nanny's day off. My folks have agreed to look after them."

She gave him a dubious look then shrugged. "Well, I guess if they survived raising you, they can survive the Beauvais."

"Very funny." He pinched her bottom through her shorts then smoothed his hand lovingly over the fullness, squeezing gently the way he might test a peach for ripeness. "How about you, *chère*?" he asked, his voice a low purr that lulled and excited her at once. "You gonna survive me?"

I don't know, Danielle thought as his mouth settled down on hers once more. And as she gave herself over to the magic of kissing him she wasn't sure she cared. When she was in his arms nothing else mattered, nothing intruded on her happiness. When he kissed her this way it didn't matter that he was younger and it was all right that she had foolishly fallen in love with him.

"You're sure this is okay?" Danielle asked, casting a worried look back at the dwindling sight of the Doucet house. "I feel guilty about it."

"Jeeze, Danielle, will you give yourself a break?" Remy fiddled with the throttle arm on the outboard motor, revving up the little engine and making the blunt-nosed *bâteau* spurt ahead in the inky water of the bayou. "My parents love havin' kids around," he yelled above the noise. "Papa will take charge of Tinks and Jeremy, Mama and Butler can handle the other three. Sit back and enjoy the ride, darlin'. Or maybe it's the idea of the swamp you don't like, *oui*?"

He held his breath as he waited for her answer. *Dieu*, was he out of his mind? Expecting a sophisticated woman like Danielle to like putting around a swamp in a little boat that reeked of fish. He was just asking to have her hand him his heart on a platter.

"Absolutely not!" Danielle insisted, offended. "After all the places I've been, I'm hardly afraid of this swamp. I've got nine rolls of film with me, and if I don't get a close-up of an alligator, I'm going to hold you personally accountable."

His grin broke across his stormy expression like the sun coming out from behind a thunderhead, and

Danielle felt her heart give a little leap. The cynic in her, the sensible star-crossed Hamilton in her, told her she was being a world-class idiot, but the tender spot Remy had touched in her soul turned a deaf ear. She smiled at him and on they went, away from Luck and the campboat, up the Bayou Noir and into the primeval world of the cypress swamp.

When they were deep in the heart of it Remy cut the engine and the mechanical buzz of the motor died off into stillness that was gradually filled by the sounds of nature. The screech of an eagle, the beating of an egret's wings, a splash, a slithering in the duckweed along the bank, the distant hoarse bellow of an alligator. He watched Danielle's face as she looked and listened, and adrenaline pumped through him at the brightness of excitement that shone in her eyes.

"It's wonderful," she whispered, loath to disturb nature with the sound of her voice. "Like the Amazon. Like the Ituri in Zaire. It's fabulous."

There was a flush on her high, perfect cheekbones. Beneath the fragile covering of her tan camisole blouse her breasts rose and fell with her shallow breaths. Her excitement was telegraphed to Remy like electric currents through the heavy air. It simmered in his blood and settled low in his belly.

With the agility of one raised on the water, he moved from his position at the back of the *bàteau* to settle on the plank seat beside Danielle, his hip brushing her hip, his shoulder nudging hers. She looked up at him and the faintest of breezes stirred a curling tendril of silvery-blond hair against her cheek. She had pulled her wild mane back and secured it with a heavy gold barrette, but almost immediately strands had escaped. Now Remy reached up with gentle fingers and brushed the curl back.

Danielle stared at him, at the smoldering passion in

his jet eyes, realizing only when her lungs started to burn that she had forgotten to breathe. She shivered a little at the thought of how powerful the pull of desire was between them. They were in the middle of a swamp, for heaven's sake, and all she could think about was having him make hot wild love with her.

He drew a bit of his lower lip between his teeth and nibbled at it as he leaned a little closer. "I love that perfume you're wearing," he murmured in a voice as dark as the bayou.

"Deep Woods Skeeter Stop," she whispered, staring at his mouth.

He sniffed and hummed appreciatively. "My favorite."

"I feel like we're the only people on earth."

"We're the only people here."

She glanced around at the lush jungle. There was something incredibly sensual, incredibly sexual about it—the wild fertile smell, the heat. "Remy . . ."

"Why not, *chère*?" he whispered, his rough voice a caress. "I missed you like hell last night." He stared at her from beneath the fringe of black lashes, his gaze as hot and relentless as the sun that lifted steam off the stagnant water. His smile was so frankly carnal it took her breath away. "*Laissez les bons temps rouler.*"

"Yeah, right," Danielle muttered. "We'll let the good times roll us right into the swamp where we will be promptly devoured by alligators."

"Don't you trust me, angel?" he asked, sliding to his knees on the floor of the boat, sliding the strap of her blouse down off her left shoulder.

"About as far as I could throw an elephant," she said, then Remy lifted her breast out of its lacy confines and took the tip of it in his mouth and all reservations were canceled by the instant rush of passion.

Danielle moaned softly and let her head fall back as

she brought her hands up to thread her fingers through his shining dark hair. Oh, how she loved the way he made her feel. Each tug of his mouth dragged a little more of her sanity away, stripped away another layer of civilized veneer.

His hand slid up under her loose cotton shirt, pushing aside the soft, sand-colored fabric to brush his fingertips against the satin skin of her inner thigh. She scooted closer to the edge of the bench, tilting her hips forward, inviting him to touch her intimately, and when he tugged aside the leg of her panties and stroked her moist heated flesh, she gasped and moaned a little bit louder.

His fingers moved slowly, rhythmically, savoring her honeyed heat. With his thumb he rubbed the tender bud of her desire as he tested the depth of her readiness, wringing another, louder moan from her. With his free hand he jerked open the front of his jeans, his manhood springing free, swollen and eager.

A sliding sensation dipped through Danielle's stomach and she realized belatedly she was slipping off the bench. Remy gathered her skirt up in fistfuls, anchoring his hands at her waist as he pulled her toward him. She curled her fingers around the back side of the seat for support and eased herself down, her knees brushing his hips as she settled on him. They both groaned as she took him deep into the hot wet silk between her legs.

Remy fastened his mouth on her nipple again and sucked strongly. Danielle panted as a raw jolt of electricity shot directly from her breast to the pit of her stomach and tightened her convulsively around his throbbing shaft, then it was Remy's turn to pant.

They made love slowly, thoroughly. With the rich wildness of nature all around them they did the most natural thing in the world, the most basic of acts between male and female, made beautiful by what was in their hearts. The passion consumed them both, building like a storm on the horizon, hotter and hotter, and when the storm broke and the passion crested, their cries of completion split the air, mingling easily with the sounds of the swamp.

They collapsed against each other, sweating and spent, gasping, lungs in search of oxygen in the sultry air. Eons passed. Danielle mustered a smattering of strength and brushed a mosquito the size of an aircraft carrier off a vital-looking vein on the back of her hand.

"I'll be eaten alive," she mumbled, her love-bruised lips brushing the shell of Remy's ear.

"Mmmm," he groaned, not stirring. "Is that a request?"

She was beyond innuendo. Her brain felt like Yorkshire pudding in her head, blitzed by the onslaught of a zillion sex-starved hormones. "There are mosquitoes out here large enough to qualify as bloodmobiles."

"Wait till you see the snakes." He lifted her back onto the bench, fastened his jeans, then dug into the cooler they'd brought along for an icy can of beer while Danielle straightened her clothes.

"I can't believe we just made love in the middle of a swamp," Danielle said, wonder in her voice and in her eyes as she took in their surroundings all over again before settling her gaze on Remy. He looked rugged and handsome sitting on the plank seat across from her, his dark face flushed. "And it felt so right," she murmured.

Remy's heart pounded against his breastbone like a fist. This was it. This was perfect.

# *Twelve*

Renard's was a combination restaurant, bar, and dance joint situated along the bank of the bayou, just down the road from the Doucets' house. Set at the edge of the woods, it was a large, unpretentious clapboard structure perched some feet off the ground on cypress stilts. The parking lot was filling up as the dinner crowd arrived.

Remy rolled his eyes and raised his arms toward heaven. "*Mon Dieu*, Danielle, come on in."

Danielle took a step backward. She felt like a fool. She'd dressed to come here, putting on a purple silk tank top and a skirt she had picked up in India that was two flowing layers of vibrant blue gauze with batik designs in soft yellow, dark blue, and fuchsia. But her enthusiasm for the night out had dwindled with every article she put on her freshly showered body. By the time she had fastened on the gold hoop earrings with the painted wooden beads, she had pretty much convinced herself she would rather just crawl under a bed and hide.

This very day the calendar page had flipped, the old

body odometer had turned over. She was forty. The sun had pinkened her face, emphasizing those tiny lines and wrinkles miracle skin cream commercials are always lamenting. She had gone over her body with the too critical eye of an artist, sure that the early signs of sagging were there. Her breasts had started to slip. In her hysterical imagination she thought she could actually see gravity dragging them down, and her butt right along with them. She'd turned and given her fanny a smack, watching in the mirror with horror, waiting for it to jiggle like an unleashed Jell-O mold.

She was a forty-year-old woman dressing up for a date with a man who thought the Supremes were soda crackers. Who was she trying to kid?

"Danielle," Remy said in his most cajoling tone. He hooked a finger through the two fine gold necklaces she wore and gently drew her close. "Come on, *chère.* I finally get a chance to take you somewhere, show you somethin', have a nice meal with no baby food involved. Come on." He gave her a lost-puppy look, tilting his head for effect.

Danielle snarled a little through her teeth as her resolve melted and her knees went weak. The blasted man knew exactly how to use all that Cajun charm to his advantage. "Oh, all right."

Remy heaved a sigh of relief, took her by the arm and led her up the steps to the door of the restaurant. The instant the screen door banged shut behind her, she knew something was terribly wrong. All the fine hairs on her arms stood on end. Remy turned her left and propelled her toward a long row of tables against the far wall and she gasped in shock and horror.

"Happy birthday, Auntie Dan-L!" Ambrose shouted, leaping in the air and flinging a fistful of confetti at her.

Tinks and Jeremy and a passel of children she'd never seen before blew on party horns until their faces turned purple, garnering the attention of everyone in the place who might by some miracle have missed the shout.

Also seated at the tables were Butler, Mama and Papa Doucet, and half a dozen other adults Danielle didn't know. All there to celebrate a birthday she would rather have skipped.

She turned around and stared up at Remy, holding herself perfectly still lest she explode into a million furious fragments. "You told these people it was my *birthday*?" She said the word with incredulous emphasis, as if he had told them her bra size.

Remy was wearing that dumbfounded-male look. "I didn't tell them which one!"

She glanced back at her party guests and gave them a wide, brittle smile, speaking right through it. "We'll be right with you, folks." Turning back to Remy, she said, "It's a shame you have to die so young."

"Oh, come on, sugar," he said with a chuckle. "All these folks want to party with you. They're all glad you were born today. I sure am glad you were born today. What difference does it make how many candles are on the cake?"

"There's a cake with *candles*?" she hissed, horrified.

"Naw." Remy winked at her. "Fire marshal wouldn't allow it."

She managed a weak laugh at that, then glanced back at the expectant faces of their dinner party. It was awfully sweet of them all to come—whoever they were. And the children looked so excited. With a little lump in her throat she thought of her last birthday, spent in Tibet with a yak and a goat.

"How old are you, Auntie Dan-L?" Ambrose asked, coming to take her hand and lead her toward the place of honor.

"Thirty-nine," she lied smoothly, murmuring under her breath, "Again."

She was promptly introduced to everyone at the table. There was Remy's oldest sister, Alicia, her husband and three children; youngest sister, Annick, who bore a striking resemblance to Remy's voodoo priestess; a couple in their sixties introduced as Tante Fanchon and Uncle Sos. Sitting to Remy's left was his twin sister, Giselle, her husband, and their twin five-year-old daughters. Absent from the Doucet brood were youngest brother, Andre, and eldest, Etienne, better known as Lucky.

With introductions out of the way everyone fell into animated conversation. Much to Danielle's relief, she discovered the Doucets pounced on the slightest reason to get together and have fun, so there was no embarrassing fuss made over her. Beyond the initial announcement and heraldry, little mention was made of the occasion, which suited her just fine.

She listened to the chatter around her, slightly distracted, her emotions in a turmoil. She studied Remy's sisters, all of them fussing happily over children. Annick, who had none of her own, had adopted Eudora for the night, much to Eudora's delight. As they waited for dinner to be served, Remy entertained two of his nieces with the G-rated version of his excursion into the swamp with Danielle.

"Auntie Danielle," Jeremy said, appearing at her side to tug at her arm. "You'll never guess what me and Tinks saw today."

"Hmm? What was that?" she asked absently, lost in her own uncertainty.

"We went into the woods with Papa Doucet and he showed us all kinds of animals and—"

"Oh, that's neat, Jeremy." She gave him a vacant smile. "But you'd better go sit down now. I think our food is coming."

"Yeah, but I want to show you—"

"Maybe later, okay?"

The boy sighed and stomped back to his seat as a pair of waitresses brought out their dinner.

Renard's was a comfortable place with natural wood paneling and big screened windows. The table-cloths were red and white checked plastic. Statues and pictures of foxes abounded. The place was doing a booming business. If the waitresses' figures were anything to go by, the meal promised to be as delicious as it smelled. Both were on the plump side with cheeks rosy from the heat in the kitchen. All the Doucets were familiar with the young women, calling them by name, asking after their families. They chatted as they served, their musically accented voices rising above the general din of plates and silverware and talk from other tables. The array of dishes was served family-style at the table.

The dish that caught Danielle's interest was the steaming platter piled high with boiled crawfish. Remy instructed her on the fine art of eating the small dark red crustaceans that looked like minia-ture lobsters, showing her how to break off the tail, crack the shell with thumb and forefinger, and dig out the rich white meat inside.

"And then," he said with a wicked gleam in his eyes. "If you're a real Cajun, you suck the fat out of the head."

"Whoa, forget it!"

"Ah, me, how we ever gonna make a Cajun outa you, *chère*?"

"You aren't if it involves sucking fat out of the head of a decapod," Danielle said dryly. "I've eaten a lot of weird stuff in a lot of weird places, but even I draw the line somewhere."

That won her a round of good-natured laughter from everyone but Remy, who merely forced a smile and sat back in his chair. He hadn't needed the reminder of her footloose lifestyle, not tonight when his heart was so set on asking her to stay forever. His stomach churned a little and it had nothing to do with the generous amounts of spicy food being served at the table. It did a barrel roll as Alicia's husband asked Danielle to tell them about some of the exotic places she'd been.

"I forgive you, *cher*," Giselle said, leaning close.

Remy looked at her as if she had just sprung up out of the ground.

His sister's eyes sparkled with the wisdom of a twin. "You're in love with her, yes?"

There was no point in denying it. Giselle was too in tune with his feelings, as he was with hers. "*Oui*," he whispered, swallowing hard.

"Then I forgive you for taking the name of my agency in vain."

"Hey," he huffed indignantly. "I'll have you know I'm a damn good nanny. I may just keep this job."

Giselle sniffed and rolled her eyes, then glanced around him at Danielle. "She's very pretty. She loves you too, yes?"

He forced a grin. "I hope so."

His twin was hardly fooled. She leaned up and kissed his cheek, her dark eyes full of understanding. For just an instant they shared an aching, uncertain heart, then Giselle smiled and said, "Poor Danielle, she's got no chance against all that charm of yours, *cher*. She'll be a Doucet before she knows it, she will."

"I hope you're right," he murmured. But as his gaze turned toward Danielle and he watched her tell a story about photographing the Efe tribe of the African Congo, all his hopes twisted into a knot of apprehension. She looked so vibrant when she spoke of those faraway places. Could he really expect her to give all that up and put down roots along the bayou when her heart had been so restless for so long?

At length the dinner plates and empty platters were cleared away by the same plump smiling waitresses.

A band took the stage on the other side of the big open room and began to tune up, plucking and sawing at fiddle strings, strumming a chord on a guitar, checking the keys of the small Evangeline accordion. The level of excitement started to rise, hitting a crescendo of clapping and whistling at the opening bars of "Allons à Lafayette."

Half the tables emptied, their occupants spilling onto the dance floor in a flood of humanity. Smiles flashed, heads bobbed, feet shuffled as they made their way around the floor in variations of the two-step. The music Danielle was beginning to love was loud and happy-sounding, the little accordion huffing and puffing between its master's hands, the triangle player bouncing with the beat, the fiddle player wailing out the French lyrics with gusto.

Danielle smiled as she listened. It was almost impossible not to move in time with the beat. As she watched the patrons of Renard's dance and laugh and chug down cold beer, she felt herself getting caught up in the atmosphere. She had been many places and seen many things, but she had fallen head over heals in love with Louisiana, with the people and the culture, the music and the land. For the first time in a long time she had begun to fantasize about staying put. It scared the hell out of her.

The raucous two-step eventually gave way to a graceful waltz. Remy rose and held a hand out to her. "How about it, sugar?"

Danielle had waltzed with princes and playboys, but their memories paled into oblivion as Remy took her in his arms. His dark eyes never left hers as he swept her around the floor, moving with a fluid natural grace no dance instructor could have taught him. Danielle found her heart fluttering and shook her head a little in amazement. The waltz was hardly a sexy dance. It was old-fashioned and formal, straight-backed and straitlaced. But she couldn't have felt more aware of Remy had they been writhing out the Lambada. And her heart swelled with love for him and her uncertainties and reservations swelled right along with it.

Like a knucklehead she'd gone and fallen in love with a younger man, a man who had pursued her with the motto of "let the good times roll." They'd had a good time. He hadn't asked for more and she would have had to have been completely obtuse to think he might ask. He was a family man, domestic for all his wily wicked charm. What would he want with her—an aging photographer with a curse on her head? She might have made an interesting diversion for the summer, but he wasn't liable to think of her as making much of a wife. No, Remy would want to look for a sweet young thing adept at cooking and cuddling babies. Cuddling a Nikon wasn't going to rank high on his list of priorities. It would probably be just below "in need of a face-lift."

Really, she thought, mentally tearing little bits off her heart, he should be looking for someone like the dark-haired little gal who was presently dancing in the corner with his twin nieces. She looked about twenty-five. Her cheeks were still slightly pudgy with the bloom of youth. Her long hair hung in a single braid down her back like a length of silken rope. The little girls she was indulging looked completely enamored of her—and she of them; as the music ended she wrapped them both in an exuberant hug. Then she looked up and caught Danielle staring and her dark eyes flashed with unmistakable dislike. Danielle frowned, unable to pull her gaze away from the acrimonious look even as Remy steered her out of the flow of traffic to the very edge of the dance floor.

"Danielle," Remy started, then choked a little as his heart leaped into his throat. He was going to do it—right here, right now—he was going to tell her. So they'd only know each other a short time, that didn't make a damn bit of difference. He was dead certain of his feelings. "Danielle," he started again. "I lo—"

"Hey, Remy!"

He squeezed his eyes shut just briefly, as if a sudden knifing pain had gone through his head. Marie. The tireless Marie. Marie the Undaunted. Marie "I Want Us to Get Married" Broussard. She couldn't have chosen a worse moment to show up if someone had given her a list of ten ways to ruin his evening.

"How about a dance, *cher*?" she said, blatantly ignoring the fact that he was holding another woman's hand.

He started to scowl at her and was about to tell her no when Danielle suddenly backed away. He looked at her, surprised and annoyed and confused. She gave him a smile as phony as a three-dollar bill and said, "Go ahead, Remy. My arthritis is acting up anyway."

Marie latched on to him with all the tenacity of a snapping turtle, her small hand clenching his in a fierce grip. She jerked him out into the throng of dancers, as purposeful as a tugboat hauling a barge up the Mississippi. He gave Danielle one last befuddled look before she disappeared from view.

Danielle stood at the edge of the crowd watching even though it was torture for her. The dark-haired young woman fit perfectly with Remy. She was petite and feminine, looking virginal and bridelike in her white sundress. She stared up at him with affection and determination.

"Auntie Danielle," Jeremy said, tugging at the leather cord of her belt. "Will you come and see now? It's so neat and I know the way and I'll bet you've never seen anything like it even in Africa."

She looked down at her nephew, perversely annoyed that he had distracted her from wallowing in self-pity. "What, Jeremy?"

"Will you come now?"

"Come where?"

"Out to see our secret."

"Jeremy, it's dark out. I'll come see it tomorrow. Why don't you go see if Tinks will dance with you?"

He regarded her with utter disgust, turned and stormed away. Danielle sighed. Another strike against her in the child-rearing category. She looked back out at the dancers, wincing as she caught sight of Remy and his little partner.

"I could look that young again," she muttered to herself. "With the aid of a belt sander and a tube of caulk."

"Oh, that Marie Broussard," Giselle said, shaking her head with disapproval as she took up the spot Jeremy had vacated. "She's been chasin' him so long you'd think her legs woulda give out by now."

Danielle's head snapped around and she had to strain to sound nonchalant. "They've known each other a long time?"

"Always. They went to school together." Giselle rolled her dark eyes and tilted her head to the angle of conspiracy and said, "You think she might have taken the hint by now. *Mais non*, she still thinks he's playin' hard to get. Some folks just need to be hit over the head with a thing, you know?"

"Yeah," Danielle whispered. "Some folks do. If you'll excuse me, Giselle, I think I'm going to step outside for a breath of fresh air."

She didn't wait for a response. She didn't even chance a look at Remy's sister for fear she might see pity in her eyes. She mowed a path to the front door and nearly stumbled down the steps in her haste to get away from the people and the music. Her sandals scuffed over the crushed shell of the parking lot as she walked out toward the bayou.

As she stared out at the black water she gave an involuntary little moan. Her feelings felt like they'd been run through a blender on puree. In the course of a matter of days they'd been jerked out of the compartment she had relegated them to, turned inside out and upside down. This was all Suzannah's fault. If it hadn't been for her half-sister, she would have right now been happily holed up in some remote corner of the world in a photographic frenzy, wearing out her Nikon shooting pictures of boulder formations and window casings. Well, "happily" might not have been the right word to use, she reflected, but at least she would have felt calm and in control. She wouldn't have been doing something stupid like falling in love with younger men.

"Hey, Danielle, where you at?"

Remy's low, rough voice came to her with all the beckoning warmth of a flannel blanket on a chill night. She wanted to wrap herself in it and shut the world out. The cynic in her sneered.

"I'm right here," she said, not turning around.

He shuffled up behind her and slid his arms around her waist, dropping his chin down on her shoulder. "Don't be ticked off at me 'cause I danced with Marie. She's like a pit bull, that one. Once she latches on it's hard to shake her."

"I'm not mad," she said flatly. "You're my nanny not my personal slave. Dance with whoever you like."

"I like you." He twirled her around to face him and pulled her into his arms for a slow dance to music he provided himself, his voice rising softly above the hum of insects and the far distant bellow of an alligator. "*Demander comme moi je t'aimais, ma jolie fille.*"

"What's that one about?" Danielle asked dryly. "Cooking muskrats on an open fire and the treachery of women?"

He tilted his head back and gave her a sober look as he translated. "'Ask how much I love you, my pretty girl.'"

"Maybe you should sing that one to the long-suffering Marie."

"I don't love Marie. I love you."

Danielle was certain her heart had stopped. Catastrophic full cardiac arrest. She swayed a little on her feet as she stared at him. He'd said it. Heaven help her. The fool in her had wanted to hear those words so desperately and now he'd said them. Now what was she supposed to do? Be selfish and grasp what he was offering or be noble and give him up for his own good?

She stared at him and considered as her emotions wrestled inside her. He was so handsome and so sweet. He made her feel things she had only read about in *Cosmo*. Did she really want to give all that up? No. She was by nature a selfish person. Hadn't she been told as much? Hadn't she drummed that idea into her own psyche over the last year? Why should she change at this late date? Why shouldn't she just throw caution and good sense to the wind and indulge herself? Why shouldn't she tell Remy she loved him?

"Remy, I—"

"Auntie Danielle!"

Danielle looked past Remy's broad shoulder to see Tinks barreling across the parking lot as fast as her little feet could fly. Her face was stark-white in the dark.

"Auntie Danielle! Come quick! Jeremy's hurt real bad!"

The emergency room of the community hospital in Luck was painted a shade of green guaranteed to make a person sick if he weren't already ill to begin with. The chairs in the waiting room were molded plastic, the floor covered with a hard gray linoleum that amplified the sound of pacing footsteps.

Danielle could not sit, unable to contain her worries to a chair. Back and forth the length of the reception desk, her arms wrapped tightly around her as if she were trying to physically hold herself together. Remy had tried to console her, but she had shrugged him off. He had finally relegated himself to a chair, pulled his cigarette out of his pocket and lit it, drawing owlish stares from his family. The entire herd of Doucets had followed the ambulance, with the exception of Giselle and her husband, who had taken all the children to Remy's parents' house to wait for word of Jeremy's condition.

*This is all my fault,* Danielle thought for the millionth time. If only she had paid more attention to Jeremy when he tried to get her to go outside with him. If only she had let him tell her the story of what he and Tinks had discovered on their nature hike with Papa Doucet. If only she hadn't been so wrapped up in her own worries, wallowing in self-pity because it was her fortieth birthday. Now, for all she knew, Jeremy might not live to see his tenth.

They had found him in the dense forest behind Renard's, unconscious, a gash in his forehead and a snake bite on the back of his small hand. He and Tinks had snuck away from the dance, bent on bringing their find to Danielle if they couldn't get Danielle to their find—an abandoned quail's nest with eggs still in it. According to Tinks, they had swiped a flashlight out of the minivan and stolen off to the woods to get the nest. Unfortunately, a copperhead had chosen the same time to make his dinner of the abandoned eggs. Jeremy had been bitten just as he'd reached for the nest. Terrified, the two children had turned and run back in the direction of Renard's, but Jeremy, possibly already feeling the effects of the snake's venom, had stumbled and fallen, striking his head.

Every time she closed her eyes Danielle could see the terrible image of her nephew, the mischief maker, the human tornado, lying so unnaturally still on the ground. And it was all her fault. Her stomach turned as she wondered how she would ever again be able to face Suzannah.

As if her thoughts had conjured up her sister, the waiting room doors slid open and Suzannah burst in with Courtland right behind her. Danielle stopped her pacing, stunned into motionlessness, and stared, thinking somewhere in the back of her mind that the pair didn't look as if they'd just come from the Caribbean. There were no signs of recent fun in the sun. They were dressed casually, as if they had just been called from a quiet evening at home. Courtland's pale hair was sticking up in back as if he might have fallen asleep on the couch while reading the newspaper. Suzannah's patrician features were scrubbed clean of cosmetics.

Suzannah rushed toward her, her flame-red hair flying behind her, her big gray eyes shadowed with worry. "Danielle! How is he? Have you heard anything?"

Danielle stared at her sister, dumbfounded. "Suzannah? Courtland? How did you get here?"

There was a flash of guilt in Suzannah's eyes as she exchanged a look with Butler, but the explanation was put on hold. The doors to the emergency room swung open and the doctor came out asking for Jeremy's parents. The trio disappeared into the nether regions of the hospital, leaving the rest of the group wondering if the news was good or bad.

Danielle wheeled on Butler, feeling she had somehow been played for a fool. "What exactly is going on here, Butler? There's no way in hell Suzannah and Courtland could have gotten here from Paradise Island in the ten minutes since you called them."

The old retainer shifted uncomfortably on his chair, his cheeks flushing to a color that nearly matched his hair. "Och, well now, lass, they werna exactly that far away."

"How far away were they *exactly*?"

Butler stared down at his shoes. "Ar—um—the Grande Belle Inn. Here in Luck since yesterday. At the Pontchartrain Hotel before that."

"There was never any trip to the islands, was there?" Danielle asked quietly.

He looked up at her and sighed, his eyes so full of pity Danielle almost couldn't bear it. "No lass. Your sister was worried. Aye, we all were worried about you. You hie yourself off to godforsaken Tibet. We see not hide nor hair of you for a year. We had to do something to get you back amongst the living. Suzannah came up with the notion of having you stay with the bairns to prove to yourself you could do it."

"To prove that I could do it," Danielle whispered, appalled and humiliated. "You made a royal fool of me. Thank you very much. And look what happened." She swung an arm in the direction of the doors to the ER. "I said from the first I was the last person Suzannah should have called on to stay with her children and I was right."

"This wasn't your fault, Danielle," Remy said, pushing himself to his feet.

"Wasn't it?" she asked, turning tortured eyes toward him.

"He'd been told not to go into the woods alone."

"He wouldn't have been alone if I had listened to him, if I had been paying attention to him instead of worrying about myself. Hell, he only wanted to impress me and I couldn't bother to pay enough attention to him to realize that."

"He wouldn't have gone out there at all if I hadn't taken him there first, *chère*," Remy's father said, his dark eyes solemn, the line of his mouth grim above his square jaw.

"You don't understand," she mumbled, tears rising up in her throat to choke her.

Remy started to put an arm around her, but she shrugged him off again. She was responsible, she should have to bear the pain alone. She'd been right to leave after the tragedy in London. She wasn't fit for the role of parent, surrogate or otherwise. In London it had been her art that had distracted her from her duty. Here it had been her love life. Either way the proof was there: she was simply too self-absorbed to be reliable in a parental situation. She belonged alone. Like many a Hamilton before her, it seemed she was destined to be alone.

She had known that for some time now, had accepted it. Then Suzannah had lured her to New Orleans and she had been given a glimpse of the life she would never have. It seemed fate had an exceedingly cruel sense of humor, she thought as she leaned a shoulder against the plate-glass window and stared out at the parking lot. During this time with the children and Remy she had been forced to dig up every emotion she had. She'd banished demons she had never wanted to face and fallen in love with a dark-haired Cajun devil who was wrong for her from the word go.

Now she would have to cram all those feelings back into their compartment like springy trick snakes in a can. For the first time ever her restless heart had longed for a home, but she was going to have to tear up the fragile roots that had already begun to grow and move on. She was going to end up playing it noble after all, she thought, her mouth twisting at the irony. She would leave the children to their parents, leave Butler to meddle in someone else's life. And she would leave Remy to that young, sweet-faced, wonderful-with-children Marie. And she would go back to the one thing she did very well or cared enough about. It was just too bad for her that her muse suddenly seemed lacking as a companion.

"Danielle, don't do this to yourself, sugar," Remy whispered.

His reflection loomed up directly behind hers in the glass, broad and strong, young and handsome. And her heart squeezed unmercifully at the thought of losing him. Oh, why couldn't they just have left her to her nomadic, solitary life? It was so much easier to live without something when you didn't know what you were missing. Now she would know and the sense of loss would be with her always.

A nurse came through the double doors to tell them that Jeremy would have to remain in the hospital for a day or two, but that he would be all right. Murmurs and sighs of relief cut through the tension in the waiting room like a sudden cooling breeze on an unbearably sultry day. Remy lifted his hands to Danielle's shoulders and rubbed at the knotted muscles.

"See?" he whispered. "He's gonna be fine."

"No thanks to me," Danielle murmured. She ducked out from under his touch and walked out of the hospital into the warm Louisiana night.

Remy started after her, but Butler called him back. "Let her go, laddie. Give her a wee moment to herself."

Remy stopped himself at the door, not altogether convinced of Butler's wisdom, but not wanting to push Danielle too hard either.

And in that wee moment Danielle slipped around to the front of the building, got into the only taxi in town, handed the driver two hundred-dollar bills, and settled in for the ride to New Orleans, leaving Luck and Remy and her heart behind.

## Thirteen

Danielle threw open the wooden shutters and stepped out onto her balcony. The scents of goats and car exhaust fumes, human sweat and cooking meat, all combined into one hot blast of air that made her think of a monkey cage at a zoo on a steamy rainy day. She staggered back into the suite and collapsed on the rattan sofa, feeling as green as new grass.

Maybe Madagascar had been a bad choice.

She had first gone to New York, but Manhattan had been too loud, the sounds too discordant. The smell of garbage smoldering on the curbs had been an affront after sweet olive and roses. Off she had flown to Paris, but the sound of Parisian French had somehow pained her heart. It lacked the warmth of its Cajun relative. And every time she turned and caught a glimpse of a man with wicked dark eyes and a black mustache her heart went into a dangerous irregular kind of rhythm. So much for France. After wandering aimlessly around Switzerland, Italy, and Greece, she had found her way to Bangkok. But the tinny sound of gongs and high-pitched oriental melodies had clashed with her idea of what a sultry night should sound like—New Orleans jazz and the basso blast of a barge horn on the river—and Bangkok had been left behind.

She had settled on Madagascar—Antananarivo, a place she couldn't even pronounce the name of—largely because she hadn't thought she could stomach a longer flight. And before she could change her mind, she had called her agent and told him she was going to do a photographic essay on lemurs. She'd been there a week and had yet to open her camera case, let alone make the necessary arrangements to go into the forest. Merrick would be peeved that no photos of lemurs were forthcoming, but Danielle couldn't work up the energy to care.

It had been two months since she'd picked up her trusty Nikon. Not since that day in the cypress swamp with Remy had she had the urge to take any photographs. All she'd really had the energy for lately was crying and throwing up. For the first time in her life her art held no appeal, offered no comfort or distraction. Her muse had been completely overwhelmed by her misery. She felt abandoned.

Never in her life had she been homesick. She had never consciously called anyplace home. But she missed Louisiana with an ache that went soul-deep. She longed for the sights, the smells, the sounds, the people. Most of all she, the perpetual loner, the independent woman of the world, missed the people she had left behind.

She had called Suzannah after her hasty departure to check on Jeremy and to apologize. Suzannah had done some apologizing of her own for duping Danielle in the first place. Danielle didn't harbor a grudge. Suzannah's heart had been in the right place. She had entrusted her children to Danielle's care to involve her with life again and to show her nothing bad would happen. Danielle was only sorry her sister's trust had been so misplaced.

Suzannah had asked her to come back, but Danielle had declined. It was better for everybody that she stay away.

News of Remy had been painfully sparse. When he had realized she'd left without so much as a goodbye, he had pulled a vanishing act of his own. Butler, having undergone a miraculous recovery from his back injury, had stayed on to help Suzannah with the children.

The children. Heaven help her, she even missed the little monsters.

Feeling the need to get really depressed, Danielle reached for the box of photographs she had been dragging around the world with her. On her flight from Luck she had stopped at the campboat just long enough to grab her camera bag, which had been loaded with memories condensed into little canisters of film. Ambrose in his Mardi Gras mask and a blue cape, sweetly innocent and strangely noble, a mysterious dog in the background. Jeremy and Tinks, eyes glowing as they contemplated a way to get into a pen full of monkeys at the zoo. Dahlia stealing a glance at her own reflection in a window, looking a little uncertain about leaving childhood behind. Little Eudora, duck fuzz hair sticking up, grinning after taking a bite out of Remy's Sno-Kone, her lips outlined in blue like a clown's makeup; Remy laughing at her, his dark face bright with the joy in his eyes. Remy pointing out a heron to Jeremy as they sat on the deck of the campboat. Remy in a rocking chair, holding the baby in his brawny arms, her head pillowed on his broad shoulder, both of them sound asleep. Remy squinting off across the bayou. Remy . . .

The tears squeezed themselves out, clinging to her lashes then rolling down her cheeks to drip onto the oversized gray T-shirt she wore. She'd never missed anybody the way she missed him. She was too old for him, too wrong in all the ways that mattered most. But her heart hadn't heeded those logical reasons. It seemed her heart was set on him being the one great love of her life and she had had to leave him behind.

"Dammit," she swore, smacking the end table with the flat of her hand in an eruption of frustration. Her soul wrung out a few more tears. She hated being noble and unselfish, giving up the only man who had ever stilled the restlessness in her. Why couldn't she have run true to form and hung on to him for her own selfish reasons?

Maybe this was the Hamilton curse resurrecting itself, making her behave out of character just to fulfill itself. Or maybe it was love. She loved Remy Doucet till she hurt right down to her toenails. Could she really have saddled him with an aging, domestically inept, career-obsessed artist when she loved him so much? No. So here she sat in the middle of Madagascar, alone.

Of course, she wasn't completely alone, technically speaking. A tiny person had taken up residence inside her. She wasn't much for conversation, but she certainly made her presence known, Danielle thought as another wave of nausea rose in her throat. A doctor had pronounced her pregnant, just shrugging when Danielle had argued the impossibility of it, as if to say "so much for the reliability of birth control."

She was carrying Remy's baby. The miracle of it awed her. The reality of it scared her spitless. Fresh tears flooded her eyes as a fresh batch of self-doubt swelled inside her like rising bread dough. She was the absolute last woman on earth who deserved to be a mother. She had proved that fact tragically.

But if she couldn't have Remy, maybe she could have this small part of him, this little person she had created with him during a night of sweet loving. She pictured the baby having his dark hair and eyes, a dimple in her plump cheek as she grinned, and Danielle thought her heart would burst with longing. Her little part of Remy, her reminder of a love that had healed her soul and brightened her life.

But who would that be fair to? She wasn't fit to raise a child on her own, and Remy, who had many times expressed his desire to be a father, would be denied the experience of knowing his own child. Her spirits plummeted again. She picked up another saltine and munched it morosely, staring unseeing at the splash of antique-gold light the morning sun spilled on the rough plaster wall across the room.

Her hand strayed to her belly and she had a sudden vision of herself rounded and heavy with child. She would have to tell Remy, of course, but she would burn to a crisp in perdition before she would give her baby to the doe-eyed Marie Broussard or any other young, incredibly pretty woman Remy chose for a wife.

Her lifestyle didn't leave room for a baby? She would change her lifestyle, she declared resolutely. Heaven knew she had lost her taste for exotic places, anyway. She would settle. Her career distracted her from other duties? She would try to cut back on the amount of work she did. She would do her best to domesticate her muse and she would hire a full-time nurse. She would be a single mother, but there was no reason she had to handle the job alone, especially when she was so afraid she would botch it. She knew her own limitations. That gave her an advantage, didn't it? She would do what every good rich girl did in the face of adversity—hire help.

Her burst of enthusiasm fizzled at the thought that there would probably be no dark-eyed Cajun rascals coming to interview for the job. Her emotions rode the roller coaster back to the bottom.

For a time after she'd fled Louisiana she had fantasized about Remy coming after her, but he hadn't. He had no doubt come to his senses, going weak with relief over his narrow escape from her. She recalled his endearing confession in the swamp after they had made love, that he was a geologist. Perhaps he'd found a job at last with an oil company.

Danielle struggled up from the low sofa, grabbed her purse off the coffee table, and headed for the door. There was no point in sitting here brooding. She could brood while she was sightseeing. Maybe Remy was gone from her life, but the rest of the world was still out there. Her stomach had settled and there was an open-air market just down the street. She'd go for a walk, find something to eat, and when she came back she would call the airlines and book a seat on the next flight headed in the general direction of the United States. She had a life to get on with, broken heart or no broken heart.

Remy barely spared a glance for the ancient sights of Antananarivo. He was dimly aware of the putty-colored houses piled up and down the steep hillsides, looking like an elaborate sandcastle city. He was acutely aware of the congestion of the traffic and he cursed under his breath as the cab slowed again. He'd been two steps behind Danielle everywhere she'd gone. He couldn't escape the urgent feeling that if he didn't get to her in the next second, he would be too late again.

He kicked himself mentally for not going after her that night at the hospital. He would have been saved a great deal of emotional turmoil and pain had he caught her there and demanded she marry him. Instead, he had let her go and then spent the next month feeling sorry for himself because she had taken off. He had wasted all kinds of time telling himself it was probably for the best because Danielle loved to travel and he couldn't bear to leave home. But home had seemed an empty, lonely place without her, and he had finally admitted he didn't want to live without her, even if it meant living in Antarctica.

The cab had stopped altogether and the cabbie was casually rolling a cigarette. This had all the earmarks of third world gridlock. Remy swore again and stuck his head out his window, trying to get a gander at the source of the problem, when a flash of silver-blond caught his eye and his heart began to race. Up ahead, half a block away, an unruly ponytail was bobbing down the street. He caught a glimpse of long legs and a camera bag and he leapt from the cab, throwing a wad of money through the window at the startled driver.

"Danielle! Hey, Danielle!"

Danielle slowed her step and shook her head, certain she was hallucinating. But the shout came again, whiskey-hoarse and masculine. The throng on the sidewalk flowed around her like a river around a boulder as she turned slowly and looked back.

"Remy," she whispered, as if saying his name louder would somehow break the spell and make him vanish.

He stopped a full six feet away from her and stood there looking rumpled and road-weary and uncertain. His eyes were bloodshot and the shadow of his beard looked blue against cheeks that were thinner than she remembered. He wore jeans and sneakers and a pale pink oxford shirt creased with the marks of sleeping in a plane seat. She had never seen anything more wonderful.

He dropped his duffle bag and said, "I don't know if I oughta kiss you or turn you over my knee for all the heartache you've caused me, *chère.*"

Danielle solved the issue by swaying unsteadily on

her feet and keeling over unceremoniously. His heart in his throat, Remy jumped to catch her.

"Danielle? Sweetheart? Are you all right?"

"What are you doing here?" she mumbled, trying to bring him into focus.

"Holdin' you," he murmured, his lips just above hers, his dark eyes intense. "And it feels pretty damn good."

"I mean, how did you find me?" The strength came back to her knees and she straightened, but Remy made no move to release her. They stood thigh to thigh, breast to chest, in the middle of the sidewalk.

"Butler tracked you down through your agent," he explained. "*Mon Dieu, chère,* you get around. It's gonna take me a while to get used to this pace."

"What do you mean?"

"I mean I love you," he murmured. "I was plenty ticked off when you split that night at the hospital without even sayin' good-bye. I went out to the swamp and stayed with my brother Lucky for a while. But the more I listened to his grumbling about how rotten women are, the more I missed you."

Danielle stared at him, bemused, not sure whether she should thank him or slap his face.

"It took me a while to get used to the idea of leavin' Lou'siana," he went on. "Leavin' my family. But the more I thought about it the more I realized how much I want *you* to be my family." He paused, screwing up his courage, giving Danielle warning that what he was about to say was momentous. "I want to marry you, Danielle."

Her head swam at the idea and for an instant Danielle was certain she was going to go down for the count, but she locked her knees and managed to remain upright. Lord, what a delicious fantasy. To marry Remy and live happily ever after. But it was just that—a fantasy.

"No, Remy," she murmured, backing out of his

embrace, shaking her head sadly. "I can't let you do that."

"Let me?" he said, incredulous, jamming his hands at his waist. He looked like a man at the frayed end of his temper. "I been chasin' you all over the ever-lovin' world! I've borrowed enough money to fly so much I've got enough Frequent Flier miles for a free trip to the moon! I finally run you to ground and you tell me you can't *let* me marry you?"

"You don't want to marry me," she said, shaking her head as she began shuffling backward toward her hotel. "I'm old and I have a curse on me. You could do lots better, Remy. Marry Marie Broussard. She seemed like a nice girl."

"Mebbe I don't want a girl. Mebbe I want a woman," he said, advancing aggressively. His hand shot out and he caught her by the wrist and hauled her up against him again. "Mebbe I don't give a fat rat's rump about some moldy old Scottish curse. I want you, angel, and I don't care if I have to go to the ends of the earth to get you. Now what do you think?"

Danielle stared up at him as all her blood drained into her feet. "I think I'm going to throw up."

"Really, Remy," Danielle said, coming out of the bathroom, her bare feet slapping on the cool tile floor. Her head was a little clearer now that she had brushed her teeth and splashed some cold water on her cheeks. She felt much more capable of talking him out of ruining his life. "I'm impossible to live with. I'm selfish and self-absorbed. I'm set in my ways, and I'm pretty sure my fanny has started to fall. Why would you want to get stuck with all that?"

Remy lounged on top of the hunter-green bed-spread, his back against the rattan headboard, a suspiciously wise gleam in his dark eyes. He gave her a lopsided smile, his dimple cutting into his cheek as he pushed himself up off the bed and sauntered toward her. "Because I love you and you love me and if your fanny's gonna fall I wanna be the one to catch it."

He wrapped his arms around her, his hands sliding down over her hips to cup her bottom through her shorts. He waggled his eyebrows. "Feels pretty good to me. What is this really all about?"

"I don't understand," Danielle whispered, suddenly serious, suddenly overcome by the emotions that had pushed her to run away in the first place. She looked up at him, her gray eyes somber and uncertain. "I don't understand why you would still want me after what happened."

"Danielle, what happened was an accident. It wasn't your fault—not what happened to Jeremy or what happened to your friend's baby. Bad things happen, sugar. Mebbe Jeremy wouldn't have gotten hurt if you'd gone with him, mebbe you would have gotten hurt instead. That would have been Jeremy's fault then, yes?"

"Well, no, of course not—"

"You're not infallible, Danielle. Everybody makes mistakes."

"I just don't want me to be one of yours," she murmured, fear and misery crowding the words in her throat and pushing at the tears behind her eyes. She loved him so much, wanted him so badly, but she wanted his happiness above her own. "I want you to be happy, Remy."

His heart gave a big thump and he felt moisture rise in his own eyes. Some selfish, self-absorbed woman she was—putting his needs first. He'd been terrified that when he finally caught up with her, he would discover that she didn't really need him, didn't really love him, that she'd been glad to get away from Louisiana and the threat of a family. But while she'd been in the bathroom tossing her cookies, he had made a quick reconnaissance of her apartment, finding the most telling evidence he could have hoped for—the photographs. Danielle unmasked her own feelings in her art, whether the picture depicted the loneliness of a closed door or her tender love for a child. What he'd seen had been emotions unfurling, longing revealed, love. So much love in that restless heart of hers just waiting for him to claim it.

He brushed a wild strand of angel's hair back from her perfect cheekbone and said, "I'll only be happy with you. Can't you see that, angel? I love you more than Lou'siana. I missed you so much I thought I'd die of it. I don't care if we have to live in Manhattan or Madagascar. Home is where the heart is, and my heart is with you, Danielle."

Two fat teardrops spilled over the dam and down her cheeks. Her soft mouth trembled. "Oh, Remy, I'd live anywhere with you if I thought it could work, but there's my muse to consider—"

"Tell your muse to move over, baby," he said on a sexy growl. " 'Cause I'm not givin' you up."

"But you're so young and—"

Remy cut her off, stepping back and holding up a hand. "We're gonna settle this age thing right here and now. You got a pen?"

"A pen?"

He nodded impatiently, spying one himself and snatching it off the night stand. He dug two fingers into the hip pocket of his jeans and produced a folded piece of paper which he opened and spread out on the small round table by the window. Danielle watched, bemused, as he pulled a small bottle of White-Out from the breast pocket of his shirt. "What is that?"

"Your birth certificate, courtesy of Butler, God bless him."

"My—?" She peered over his shoulder as he pulled the little brush out of the White-Out and stroked it with an artistic flourish over the year of her birth. "You can't do that!"

Remy grinned like a pirate. "Why not? Loosen up, *chère*. Let the good times roll!"

Danielle laughed, caught between hysteria and bliss, as Remy took up the pen and carefully inked in 1960.

"There you go, darlin'. We are now officially the same age." He rose and handed her the document, his dark eyes sparkling with wicked merriment.

Danielle looked down at the paper in her hand and smiled. "Gee, I feel younger already."

Remy slid his arms around her waist and started a slow dance to some secret music in his head. "Do you feel like gettin' married?"

She looked at him, amazed and in love. The man was determined; who was she to argue? He was handsome and sexy and wicked and wise beyond his years. She would have had to have been an idiot to give all that up. "Yeah, I do," she murmured, swaying in time with him.

Remy pulled her closer and kissed her, savoring the taste of her as if she were his first and last sip of a life-giving elixir. Danielle wound her arms around his neck and basked in the joy of touching him again. She felt renewed. The glow of love filled her with golden warmth. Her heart swelled in her breast as she thought of telling him about the baby . . . later . . . after they'd given each other a proper lover's welcome.

"You know," Remy said, lifting his head just enough to speak. "I suddenly feel in need of a long, long shower."

Danielle gave him a sultry, sexy look. "You need any help with that, *cher*?"

"Oh, yeah," he drawled, his dark eyes dancing. "Absolutely."

# THE EDITOR'S CORNER

What a joy it is to see, hear, smell and touch spring once again! Like a magician, nature is pulling splendors out of an invisible hat—and making us even more aware of romance. To warm you with all the radiance and hopefulness of the season, we've gathered together a bouquet of six fabulous LOVESWEPTs.

First, from the magical pen of Mary Kay McComas, we have **KISS ME, KELLY,** LOVESWEPT #462. Kelly has a rule about dating cops—she doesn't! But Baker is a man who breaks the rules. In the instant he commands her to kiss him he seizes control of her heart—and dares her to tell him she doesn't want him as much as he wants her. But once Kelly has surrendered to the ecstasy he offers, can he betray that passion by seducing her to help him with a desperate, dirty job? A story that glows with all the excitement and uncertainties of true love.

With all things green and beautiful about to pop into view, we bring you talented Gail Douglas's **THE BEST LAID PLANS,** LOVESWEPT #463. Jennifer Allan has greenery *and* beauty on her mind as she prepares to find out exactly what Clay Parrish, an urban planner, intends to do to her picturesque hometown. Clay is a sweet-talker with an irrepressible grin, and in a single sizzling moment he breaches Jennifer's defenses. Once he begins to understand her fears, he wages a glorious campaign to win her trust. A lot of wooing . . . and a lot of magic—in a romance you can't let yourself miss.

In Texas spring comes early, and it comes on strong—and so do the hero and heroine of Jan Hudson's **BIG AND BRIGHT,** LOVESWEPT #464. Holt Berringer is one of the good guys, a long lean Texas Ranger with sin-black eyes and a big white Stetson. When the entrancing spitfire Cory Bright has a run-in with some bad guys, Holt admires her refusal to hide from threats on her life and is determined to cherish and protect her. Cory fears he will be too much like the domineering macho men she's grown to dislike, but Holt is as tender as he is tough. Once Cory proves that she can make it on her own, will she be brave enough to settle for the man she really wants? A double-barrelled delight from the land of yellow roses.

Peggy Webb's **THAT JONES GIRL**, LOVESWEPT #465, is a marvelous tale about the renewal of an old love between a wild Irish rover and a beautiful singer. Brawny wanderer Mick Flannigan had been Tess Jones's first lover, best friend, and husband—until the day years before when he suddenly left her. Now destiny has thrown them together again, but Tess is still too hot for Mick to handle. She draws him like a magnet, and he yearns to recapture the past, to beg Tess's forgiveness . . . but can this passion that has never died turn into trust? For Peggy's many fans, here is a story that is as fresh, energetic, and captivating as a spring morning.

Erica Spindler's enchanting **WISHING MOON**, LOVESWEPT #466, features a hero who gives a first impression that belies the real man. Lance Alexander seems to be all business, whether he is hiring a fund-raiser for his favorite charity or looking for a wife. When he runs into the cocky and confident Madi Muldoon, she appears to be the last person he would choose to help in the fight to save the sea turtles—until she proves otherwise and he falls under the spell of her tawny-eyed beauty. Still Lance finds it hard to trust in any woman's love, while Madi thinks she has lost her faith in marriage. Can they both learn that wishes made on a full moon—especially wishes born of an irresistible love for each other—always come true? A story as tender and warm as spring itself.

In April the world begins to move outdoors again and it's time to have a little fun. That's what brings two lovers together in Marcia Evanick's delightful **GUARDIAN SPIRIT**, LOVESWEPT #467. As a teenager Josh Langly had been the town bad boy; now he is the local sheriff. When friends pair him with the bewitching dark-haired Laura Ann Bryant for the annual scavenger hunt, the two of them soon have more on their minds than the game.

Forced by the rules to stay side by side with Josh for a weekend, Laura is soon filled with a wanton desire for this good-guy hunk with the devilish grin. And though Josh is trying to bury his bad boy past beneath a noble facade, Laura enchants him beyond all reason and kindles an old flame. Another delectable treat from Marcia Evanick.

And (as if this weren't enough!) be sure not to miss three unforgettable novels coming your way in April from Bantam's spectacular new imprint, FANFARE, featuring the best in women's popular fiction. First, for the many fans of Deborah Smith, we have her deeply moving and truly memorable historical **BELOVED WOMAN**. This is the glorious story of a remarkable Cherokee woman, Katherine Blue Song, and an equally remarkable frontiersman Justis Gallatin. Then, making her debut with FANFARE, Jessica Bryan brings you a spellbinding historical fantasy, **ACROSS A WINE-DARK SEA**. This story has already wowed *Rendezvous* magazine, which called Jessica Bryan "a super storyteller" and raved about the book, describing it as "different, exciting, excellent . . ." The critically-acclaimed Virginia Brown takes readers back to the wildest days of the Wild West for a fabulous and heartwarming love story in **RIVER'S DREAM**.

All in all, a terrific month of reading in store for you from FANFARE and LOVESWEPT!

Sincerely,

*Carolyn Nichols*

Carolyn Nichols,
Publisher,
LOVESWEPT
Bantam Books
666 Fifth Avenue
New York, NY 10103

# THE LATEST IN BOOKS
# AND AUDIO CASSETTES

## Paperbacks

| | | | |
|---|---|---|---|
| ☐ | 28671 | **NOBODY'S FAULT** Nancy Holmes | $5.95 |
| ☐ | 28412 | **A SEASON OF SWANS** Celeste De Blasis | $5.95 |
| ☐ | 28354 | **SEDUCTION** Amanda Quick | $4.50 |
| ☐ | 28594 | **SURRENDER** Amanda Quick | $4.50 |
| ☐ | 28435 | **WORLD OF DIFFERENCE** Leonia Blair | $5.95 |
| ☐ | 28416 | **RIGHTFULLY MINE** Doris Mortman | $5.95 |
| ☐ | 27032 | **FIRST BORN** Doris Mortman | $4.95 |
| ☐ | 27283 | **BRAZEN VIRTUE** Nora Roberts | $4.50 |
| ☐ | 27891 | **PEOPLE LIKE US** Dominick Dunne | $4.95 |
| ☐ | 27260 | **WILD SWAN** Celeste De Blasis | $5.95 |
| ☐ | 25692 | **SWAN'S CHANCE** Celeste De Blasis | $5.95 |
| ☐ | 27790 | **A WOMAN OF SUBSTANCE** Barbara Taylor Bradford | $5.95 |

## Audio

☐ **SEPTEMBER** by Rosamunde Pilcher
Performance by Lynn Redgrave
180 Mins. Double Cassette    45241-X    $15.95

☐ **THE SHELL SEEKERS** by Rosamunde Pilcher
Performance by Lynn Redgrave
180 Mins. Double Cassette    48183-9    $14.95

☐ **COLD SASSY TREE** by Olive Ann Burns
Performance by Richard Thomas
180 Mins. Double Cassette    45166-9    $14.95

☐ **NOBODY'S FAULT** by Nancy Holmes
Performance by Geraldine James
180 Mins. Double Cassette    45250-9    $14.95

---

**Bantam Books, Dept. FBS, 414 East Golf Road, Des Plaines, IL 60016**

Please send me the items I have checked above. I am enclosing $_____
(please add $2.50 to cover postage and handling). Send check or money order,
no cash or C.O.D.s please. (Tape offer good in USA only.)

Mr/Ms _____

Address _____

City/State _____ Zip _____

Please allow four to six weeks for delivery.
Prices and availability subject to change without notice.

FBS—1/91